ONE CHRISTMAS PICKLE

A MULBURY MYSTERY NOVELLA

JUNO HARVEY

First published by Mandurang Press 2021

Book cover by Melissa Williams Design

ISBN: 978-0-6452604-3-4 (ebook)

ISBN: 978-0-6452604-4-1 (paperback)

To Michelle (now you've got time to read)

ONE

Rosemary Exeter adjusted the blind on the skylight to block out more sunlight. The move darkened the interior of The Preserved Mulbury but didn't make it any cooler. She turned the ceiling fans up as fast as they could go without blowing the jam jars off her shelves and stood underneath one to catch the breeze. 'Hasn't been this hot in December for years,' she remarked to Sunny, who watched her from the entrance to Rosemary's living area. *You should try wearing a fur coat,* the ginger tabby seemed to say as she disappeared back inside to lie on the cool slate floor.

Outside, the tiny tourist town of Mulbury was nearly empty. A lone figure stood under the shade of The Exceptional Tree in the middle of Goldmarket Square, fanning herself with the paper bag from a pie. Despite the scorching day, visitors couldn't resist Franco's patisserie products, not even his hot pastries. Rosemary noticed that the visitor also clutched an iced tea from Kelly's café.

The door jangled open, and Mrs Lionel stepped in, brushing the back of her hand across her forehead. 'Hello, dear,' she said, pushing the door firmly shut behind her. 'I hoped that your shop was cooler than mine.'

'Any luck there?'

'No.' The older woman shifted her collar away from the back of her neck. 'At least we're protected from the worst of it by the veranda. And these lovely old brick buildings stay much cooler than those modern architectural monstrosities.' She looked around. 'Do you have plenty of stock for the Christmas holiday period?'

Rosemary nodded. 'Lots of jams, jellies, pickles, dried and brandied fruit in the cellar. A little short on marmalade, surprisingly, as I made so much over winter. It was very popular.'

'That's good. At least you don't have to make more during this heat.' Mrs Lionel pushed at her soft, grey curls. 'It's melting my soaps.'

'Come and have a cold drink.' Rosemary indicated the doorway. 'I made up some lemon cordial this morning. The shops will be okay unattended for a while. We won't get many tourist buses in today.'

'True.' Mrs Lionel followed Rosemary into the dim kitchen. 'The oldies won't want to come out on a forty-degree day.'

Rosemary turned so that Mrs Lionel wouldn't see her quick smile. The *oldies* that Mrs Lionel referred to were often younger than Mrs Lionel herself. 'Probably not tomorrow, either, as it's forecast to be as hot as today or even hotter. It's a shame, tomorrow being Christmas Eve. I thought we might get some last-minute sales.'

Mrs Lionel took the glass that Rosemary offered. 'What about this for an idea? We could open early when the day is at its coolest. Really early, if we must. During heat waves like this, most people like to do things before ten o'clock in the morning but that's when we usually open. It's rather silly of us being open in the afternoon, like we are now.'

'Yes. Great idea.' Rosemary drained the last of her drink and put her glass in the sink. 'We could advertise early opening. *Mulbury Mornings.*'

'Mulbury Mornings. I like it a lot. Do you think seven o'clock is too early?'

'Not for us. Not for Jasper or Patti, either.' Rosemary nodded towards the shops on the other side of the adjoining wall. 'Rakisha won't like it.'

'We could help her out. And she could have a nap in the afternoon. The poor dear. It must be hard being a night owl.'

Rosemary said nothing. *Night owl* was not even remotely in her imagination.

'Doing some cleaning up?'

Rosemary looked where Mrs Lionel was pointing. A drawer on her sideboard hung open, revealing a cascade of unopened letters. She hurried to it and slid it shut with her hip. 'No. Rearranging.'

'Ah.' Mrs Lionel sipped at her drink. 'Anything you want to talk about?'

'No.' Rosemary gave her friend a wry smile. 'Not now.'

'When you're ready.' Mrs Lionel handed her empty glass over. 'Perhaps if you tidied them up, you'd feel better.' She patted her own forehead. 'I'm cooler now. Thank you, dear. I must go back.' She pointed at where Rosemary's plum pudding hung in its calico bag from the beam in the walk-in pantry. 'How many breadcrumbs did you put in this time?'

'Four cups.'

Mrs Lionel shook her head. 'Still too much, dear. I always put in a tad under three and a half cups.'

Rosemary titled her head. 'Well,' she said, 'the proof of the pudding is always in the eating.'

Mrs Lionel nodded. 'Oh, yes, indeed.'

As the older woman returned to The Green Mulbury, Rosemary glanced once more at the sideboard and cast its contents from her mind. Instead, she made her way to Jasper Lu's bookshop. She pushed at the heavy door. It eventually opened with a sigh to reveal Jasper sitting on the floor at the base of a bookshelf, his long black hair in an untidy man-bun. From Jasper's living area came the soft snores of Snowy, his ancient dog, that spent his life mainly on the couch. Rosemary coughed pointedly. 'Looking for something?' she said.

Jasper glanced up, the open book in his hand and the dreamy look on his face showing that he'd been completely lost in a story. *Another Regency romance,* thought Rosemary.

'Hello, Rosemary.'

'How is Miss Middleton?'

Jasper's mouth dropped open slightly as he struggled to speak. 'Miss...? Oh. How did you...?'

'Isn't she your favourite heroine?'

He ducked his head, but she still saw the colour race into his cheeks. 'In my book world. I have another in real life.'

Rosemary didn't ask who he meant, although she had a pretty good idea. Jasper spent another long moment studying the floor until he scrambled up, long legs hitting the shelves as he did. 'I've come with a proposal,' she said.

If he'd been crimson faced before, it was nothing compared to the scarlet wash that flooded his face now. 'Oh.'

'Jasper, really.' Rosemary crossed her arms. 'Mrs Lionel

and I would like to open our shops earlier to get people to visit Mulbury before the heat of the day. What do you think?'

'That's a great idea.' Jasper placed a bookmark carefully into his novel and set it on top of a shelf. 'The last couple of days have been dead. I've sold exactly two thrillers and one set of Christmas cooking books in forty-eight hours. Not exactly raking it in.'

'What about your online sales?'

'They're better, although people prefer to give others new books for Christmas rather than second-hand ones.' He shrugged. 'Doesn't really matter. I'll get rushed off my feet in January when the holiday crowds hit us.'

'Right. Mulbury Mornings it is.' Something outside caught Rosemary's eye, and she craned her neck around to see through Jasper's shaded windows. 'Fire truck.'

'What?' Jasper threaded his way quickly through his books to the door. 'Not a bushfire nearby, I hope?'

A large older model fire truck pulled up in Goldmarket Square. It was a deep rusty maroon with a rounded bonnet, making it look like an ancient cousin to the square, tangerine-coloured newer trucks seen frequently dashing back and forth from Big Town at the height of fire season. Although the body of the truck had a fire hose looped around hooks on its side, the hose was flat and dirty. *More presentation than practical,* Rosemary thought. Four figures sat in the cabin, and from the exaggerated gestures of several arms, they were arguing. 'Not a bushfire or they wouldn't be stopping in the Square.' Rosemary went to the door. 'Let's ask.'

Jasper had to hurry as she crossed Goldmarket Road to the Square. She saw him striding up next to her as she reached the gravelly surface of the centre of Mulbury and smiled. His man-bun had shaken loose, and hair spilled down his back. Before she could point it out to him, the door of the fire truck opened, and Santa Claus spilled out.

Rosemary halted. 'I get it now.'

'You do?' Jasper shaded his eyes against the glare of the sun off the truck. 'A Santa steps out of a fire truck and you *get it*?'

Rosemary glanced at him. 'I forget you were raised in the city. In country towns, Santa always came to visit in a fire truck and handed out sweets to the children. In the meantime, the other firefighters rattled tins for money collection. It was really a fundraiser for the country fire brigades, all of which are manned by volunteers, but we thought it was an actual visit from Santa.'

'And did those Santas look like this one?' Jasper tipped his head towards the truck. 'Aren't they meant to be jolly and nice?'

Rosemary turned her attention back to the fire truck. The other fire volunteers were out of the cabin and were standing a little distance from the Santa. *He doesn't look the least jolly or nice,* she thought. *In fact, he looks livid.*

Santa was wearing an enormous red and white jacket that had clearly been padded to make him rounded. From his face hung a scruffy white beard on loose elastic that looked like a rodent had eaten it. Skinny wrists and gnarled knuckles thrust out of the jacket's sleeves, and a balding head protruded from the faux fur neckline. His face was a deeper shade of russet than the truck, and his eyes were bloodshot. He fiddled with the zip at his neck but couldn't locate the tag to unfasten it.

'Leave it, Ivan,' said one of the fire volunteers, a man casually eating an apple. 'A short drive up the road and we'll be there.'

'Listen to Dennis, Ivan. You don't want to scare the

kiddies by putting on a Santa suit where they can see you,' said another, a tall woman wearing aviator sunglasses.

'Yeah, Ivan.' The third fire officer took a long drink from a bottle of water. 'Not far to go.'

'Give me that, Clive.' Ivan tore the beard off, flung his hand out and snatched the bottle away before emptying it with long, loud gulps. He threw it back. 'It's alright for you lot.' He clawed at the neck of the jacket. 'You're only in T-shirts. It's roasting in this jacket.'

'Well, yes, but you volunteered to be Santa this year,' said Clive, pushing the empty bottle into the pocket on his cargo pants.

'I didn't know it was going to be over forty degrees by lunchtime.' Ivan pulled at the front of his suit. 'Since when did this outfit get so heavy?'

'Since you got so old,' said the woman, grinning. 'I wore it last year, and it was okay.'

Ivan eyed her. 'Right, Claudia. Aren't you only one year younger than me?' He shook himself, trying to get the material away from his skin, noticing Rosemary and Jasper at the same time.

'Hi,' said Jasper, lifting one hand in greeting.

'You're too old.'

'Pardon?'

Ivan waved his hand. 'If you're looking for handouts, I only give them out to children.'

'But you can donate to a good cause.' Clive went back to the truck and pulled out an electronic payment device. 'We're raising money to get a new truck.'

Jasper glanced at Rosemary. 'I thought you said they rattled collection tins?'

Clive laughed. 'Welcome to the modern world, my friend.'

As Jasper fished around in his wallet for his card, the Square's population rose. Rakisha came out of The Sweet Potato, her wild hair swept to the top of her head and held loose with a bandana so that she resembled an unfurled umbrella. Kelly walked from Mullings of Mulbury, a large straw hat shrouding her face. Mrs Lionel stepped up beside Rosemary, having crossed the road clutching a jug of iced water and a stack of cups.

'That will be welcome,' said Rosemary.

'Oh, yes, thank you, darling.' Rakisha plucked a cup from the stack and reached for the jug. 'I've had such a morning. I broke my wooden spoon stirring my mixture, and it's so hot baking oatmeal biscuits that I almost expired!'

'Then stop baking.' Kelly tipped her sunglasses down to glare at Rakisha over their top. 'That would be the intelligent thing to do.'

'Well, yes, darling, but you see I've completely run out of sweeties and my customers do so love my wholesome cookies.'

Kelly laughed. 'How can they? They're so bitter.'

Rakisha tossed her head, making tendrils of hair flutter around. 'Not bitter, darling. *Unsweetened.*' She flicked a particularly long hair out of her eyes. 'Not loaded with unhealthy sugars like some people around here stuff into their cooking.'

'Right,' said Mrs Lionel, stepping forward and taking the water back from Rakisha. 'Enough of that. I was going to offer a drink to our friends here. Would you like one?'

Claudia raised her hand. 'Yes, please. This is very nice of you.'

'I've done my fair share of fundraising in the past.' Mrs Lionel handed her the jug. 'I know what it's like.' She stared at Ivan, who was still clutching at his jacket. 'Are you alright?'

'Hot.' Ivan grabbed the jug off Claudia and tipped its contents over his head. 'Hot.'

The cold water dripping over his face made no difference to the startling scarlet of his head. Mrs Lionel stepped forward in alarm as Ivan tilted toward her, his arms windmilling wildly. Jasper jumped in to catch him at the same time as Clive, so they banged uselessly together. Rosemary was the one to grab, then lower Ivan to the ground.

'Hot,' he said, his eyes rolling up in his head.

'Oh!' said Rakisha. 'Oh, darling, is he alright?'

Rosemary held the man as Mrs Lionel checked his pulse. 'No,' said the older woman, gesturing for Rosemary to lie Ivan flat.

Jasper knelt as well, so Ivan was surrounded. Mrs Lionel sat back and the three Mulburians glanced at each other. 'Mrs Lionel?' whispered Jasper. 'What do you think?'

She shook her head. 'We'd better start resuscitation. Otherwise, he's dead.'

TWO

Within seconds, the remaining fire volunteers had nudged the others aside and started first aid on the stricken Ivan. Rosemary swept up the Santa suit jacket as they peeled it off him and stepped back to give the workers space. They had a portable defibrillator on Ivan's chest listening to its commands, but Mrs Lionel still looked grim. Jasper called the ambulance, and the townspeople kept well back as it arrived. After a tense assessment, the paramedics loaded Ivan onto the trolley and sped back to Big Town, leaving the firefighters in a sad huddle around their truck, talking to their home base through their radio.

'He's not going to make it, is he?' asked Jasper.

'No, dear.' Mrs Lionel sighed. 'But the paramedics have to keep trying until they call it.'

'What do you mean, darling?' said Rakisha, her face pale.

'They have to wait until they're absolutely sure his heart won't start. Then they call it, meaning they declare him dead.'

'Oh.' Jasper finally noticed the loose hair trailing down

his back and twisted it into the man-bun again. 'I guess you've seen lots of nearly dead people.'

'Nurses do. It was part of my everyday when I worked in the trauma ward many years ago.' Mrs Lionel shook her head. 'Doesn't make it easier.'

'How dreadful, darling.' Rakisha shivered. 'So terrible.'

'You don't look right, Rakisha.' Kelly put a hand on the other woman's arm. 'Come and sit down in my café. Cooler than yours.'

'Thank you, Kelly, darling. I do feel quite...'

'Shattered is how you look.' Kelly steered Rakisha away, looking back over her shoulder to Rosemary. 'Come and rescue me in ten minutes. I don't want to be stuck...' she pointed her chin towards her charge.

Rosemary gave a short nod as the women left the Square. 'Just when I thought Kelly was being kind.'

'She was, in her own way,' said Mrs Lionel, gathering her cups from the ground where they'd fallen during the chaos.

Jasper bent to retrieve the jug. 'How awful. Santa dying in our Square just before Christmas.'

'Awful at any time,' said Rosemary, studying the jacket in her arms.

'Well, yes, but particularly awful right now.' He ran a hand over his face. 'What do you think he died from?'

'Hyperthermia,' said Rosemary.

'It must have been so hot in that jacket.'

'Hot and then some.' Rosemary held the Santa suit up. 'See this?' She turned the material inside out.

'That's not an ordinary suit.' Mrs Lionel squeezed it in several places. 'It seems to have extra lining.'

'Can I see?' Jasper took the jacket from Rosemary and felt around it until he came to something at its back. 'Batteries.' He held the material firm and Rosemary saw the outline of two hard rectangles. 'This is a heated jacket.'

'A heated jacket?' Mrs Lionel held her palm against it. 'It feels hot, but it is a hot day.'

'It's hotter than it should be, even on a day like this.' Jasper passed the jacket back to Rosemary. 'Someone's stitched the Santa suit onto one of those outdoor vests that people buy to keep warm in the winter. There are coils in it that are heated by batteries.'

'He was wearing a heated jacket on one of the hottest days of the year.' Mrs Lionel frowned. 'Perhaps he didn't notice it was on.'

'That's not the issue, though.' Rosemary held the jacket up to her cheek, feeling the heat radiate onto her already very hot skin. 'Why would a Santa suit, traditionally worn in the heat of an Australian summer, be lined with a heated vest?'

'Perhaps someone wore it for a Christmas in July celebration?' Jasper said.

'Not likely. No one has Christmas in July outside. If they hold it at all, it's because they want to eat roast turkey in the middle of the year with everyone seated around a dining room table and a roaring fire in the background.' She shook her head. 'No, this was something else.'

'Are you saying,' said Jasper slowly, 'that someone wanted to cook Santa inside his own suit?'

Rosemary looked at Mrs Lionel, who raised her eyebrows. 'It's looking exactly like that.'

'Excuse me.'

Rosemary turned at the voice to see Clive standing behind them, his eyes puffy. She glanced back at the other members of the fire team, folding the jacket into a small parcel as she did.

'We've just heard. Ivan's dead.'

Rosemary nodded slowly while Mrs Lionel reached out for the man's shoulder and gave it a squeeze. After a moment, Rosemary said, 'You look terrible. Come inside for a while.' She pointed to her shop.

'We thought we'd better get going...' Clive's shoulders drooped.

'Yes. Soon. Looks like Ivan wasn't the only one who's become too hot.' She beckoned to Claudia and Dennis. 'Inside.'

She assumed by the sound of their weary boots on the gravel that they had followed Mrs Lionel, Jasper and her. Jasper held the front door of The Preserved Mulbury as everyone trooped in, making Sunny lash her tail at the sudden influx of people to her territory. She stalked to the window and jumped elegantly onto the sill, glaring at the crowd.

Rosemary pointed to the couch, and the three fire fighters sank heavily into it. Mrs Lionel rinsed the jug at the sink and filled it with lemon cordial while Jasper sat on the edge of an armchair. No one spoke until Mrs Lionel had set the jug and fresh glasses on the coffee table and taken her seat. Rosemary kept standing, but not before she hung the Santa jacket out of sight on a rack behind her winter coat.

'I can't believe it,' said Claudia. She put her elbows on her knees and leaned her forehead into her palms. 'That cranky old man is gone.'

Dennis stretched his arms over his head. 'Can't say I'll miss him.'

'Dennis,' said Clive severely. 'Have a heart.'

'Yeah, I'm sorry and all that, but he was a cantankerous old b-'

'That'll do,' said Claudia. 'We all have faults.'

Dennis eyed her. 'Some more than others.'

'Did he always play Santa?' said Rosemary.

'No,' said Ivan. 'It was his turn. Fifteen years we've been playing Santa to raise money for a new truck. Fifteen years of fundraising and the price of trucks goes up faster than we can save. We rotate Santa every year.'

Jasper glanced at Rosemary. 'You don't know about-'

She cut him off with a movement of her hand. 'Ivan wasn't well liked.'

'No one should speak ill of the dead,' said Claudia, crossing her arms over her chest.

'Not all the dead deserve to be spoken well of,' said Dennis.

'You see,' said Clive, 'he wasn't well liked. But that's not the same as wishing him dead.'

Rosemary raised one eyebrow. 'You wished him dead.'

'No! No. That's not what I meant.' Clive waved his hands at the others. 'What I meant was we wouldn't wish that anyone on our team was dead. We're a volunteer fire brigade and we need all the members we can get.'

Rosemary moved to perch on the arm of Mrs Lionel's chair. The three fire volunteers had their heads down. Claudia's arms were still firmly crossed, and her aviators perched precariously on top of her wavy hair. Dennis had his hands on his knees, gripping them tightly so his knuckles whitened. Clive was the most relaxed, but Rosemary saw him wipe a rough hand across his eyes.

'I'll nip back to my shop, dear,' said Mrs Lionel as the silence went on. 'Let me know if you want anything.'

Rosemary helped her friend up and watched as she went through the shop and out the jangling door. The faint croak of the electronic frog at the door of The Green

Mulbury told her Mrs Lionel was back inside. 'Jasper, do you need to go as well?'

He shook his head. 'I'm fine.'

'But *we* should get going.' Clive stood, taking a moment to tug down his shirt and smooth the wisps of his silver hair back. 'We'll have to break the news to the ones that haven't heard.'

'That's hard,' said Jasper. 'Did Ivan have a big family?'

'He didn't have anyone.' Claudia pushed herself off the couch. 'An ex-wife from a long time ago. No children. He lived alone, always had as long as I can remember.'

'He lived next to you, Claud.' Dennis gave a sudden grin. 'No more fights over the fence.'

'He fought you over the fence?' said Jasper.

'He was always yelling this and that over the fence. Shut the dog up. Shut the grandchildren up. Stop singing. Stop that lawnmower.' Claudia shrugged. 'Like I said: *cranky*.'

'He tried to poison your dog,' said Dennis, rocking back and forth before he could finally heave himself up.

'Maybe. The dog was sick. He could have eaten an old bone, for all we know.'

'Or Ivan could've poisoned him.'

'That's why none of you liked him.' Rosemary moved to let the fire volunteers through. 'He was unnecessarily cranky, and he poisoned a dog.'

'Allegedly. Those, and other things.' Dennis pointed to Clive. 'He spread rumours about you.'

Clive shook his head. 'Nothing came of it.'

'Yeah? And he stole fundraising money from the brigade.' Dennis held up his hand to stop the others from speaking. 'Don't deny it. As treasurer, I know he did.'

'He was a law unto his own,' said Claudia. She glanced

through the doorway to the shelves of The Preserved Mulbury. 'Nice stuff you've got in here. I should buy some last-minute Christmas presents.'

'Feel free,' said Rosemary.

'I'll get some money from the truck.' She stood slowly and tromped through the shop before jangling out the door.

'Feel that heat even from here?' said Dennis as the door closed. 'I'm not looking forward to going out there.'

'I thought you'd be used to the heat,' said Jasper. 'I mean, you're, you know, *fire fighters.*'

'Fighting fires is not my day job.' Dennis shrugged. 'And I usually stick to radio communications when one's on.'

'What do you do for a day job?' Jasper indicated the wall behind Rosemary's kitchen. 'I run the bookstore next door, The Read Mulbury.'

'Nice,' said Dennis. 'Don't mind a book or two around the house. I'm a builder normally. Work for myself with a couple of blokes helping.' He pointed his thumb at Clive. 'He's a meat inspector in an abattoir, and Claudia runs the dairy section of the supermarket in Big Town. We've been volunteer fire fighters for over fifteen years.'

'With Ivan?'

'He turned up somewhere along the way. Lost his job and moved to the country. Been very involved with the brigade. A bit too involved, some would say.' Dennis thrust his hands into his trouser pockets and shook his head. 'Poor fellow. Nasty way to go, overheating.'

'We worry about that, don't we, Dennis?' Clive wriggled his shoulders. 'Well, we worry when we've got our fire-fighting clobber on and it's really hot. We have to make sure we drink lots of water and take breaks if we can.'

'Did Ivan?' said Rosemary.

'What?'

'Did Ivan drink enough water today?'

Clive shrugged. 'Don't know. Maybe not.'

Claudia jangled back into the shop and started plucking jars from the shelf. Dennis beckoned to Clive, and they stood to join Claudia in the shop, although they took no notice of the displayed produce. Rosemary followed them to the shop counter and watched the men as she stacked jars into a bag and accepted Claudia's payment. Clive and Dennis looked red-faced and weary, but then so did everyone who'd suffered through the last week of intense summertime temperatures. Claudia took her bag and Rosemary noted her hand was shaking.

'Come on,' said Dennis. 'Let's get an iced coffee before we head back.' He lifted his hand to Rosemary. 'Thanks for the drink and the chance to cool down.' He nodded to Jasper.

Rosemary crossed her arms as they filed out the door.

'I know that look,' said Jasper, coming over to the shop counter as the door jangled closed. 'What are you thinking, Rosemary Exeter?'

'I don't know what you mean, Jasper Lu.'

'Yes, you do.' He put a hand on the counter, so it rested close to hers. 'You think that someone deliberately lined the Santa suit with a heated vest.'

Rosemary slid her hand back. 'Clearly.'

'Which means...?' Jasper's dark gaze didn't leave her face.

She matched his hard stare. 'You know it as well as I do. Ivan was murdered.'

THREE

Despite the heat and the presence of the truck as a russet reminder of the sad event of the day, Mulbury ticked on towards evening. Rosemary stayed in her shop leafing through Aunt Lilibeth's recipe book to be reminded of typical summer conserves. It was too early in the season for a surplus of tomatoes, eggplants or capsicum, so Rosemary's stores were stagnant. She decided to enjoy the lull, knowing that a cascade of fruit and vegetables would come her way soon enough, and closed the old book carefully.

The door jangled open. Mrs Lionel peered around it. 'Rosemary, there's something here for you.'

Rosemary walked to the door, the breeze from the ceiling fans tugging at the hair in her long braid as she passed under them. She smoothed the strands down as she reached her friend. 'What do you mean?'

'On the doorstep.'

Mrs Lionel moved aside. A large, brown package balanced precariously on the old sandstone step, tied with a fussy red and green array of ribbons. Written on the brown paper in thick black pen was *One Christmas pickle for you, Rosemary*.

'Who put it there?'

'It's a mystery, dear.' Mrs Lionel bent over to look more closely at the package. 'A Christmas pickle, as it says.'

'I didn't see anyone. I was reading.' Rosemary squatted down to the package. 'A Christmas present.'

'An early one.' Mrs Lionel straightened with a faint groan. 'You can't open it until Christmas day.'

'No.' Rosemary picked the present up, feeling the weight. 'Large but light.'

'It could be from a customer.'

Rosemary thought of the loyal customers that came every few weeks to stock up on their jams. 'No. They would have brought it in.'

'Well, I don't know, dear, but it can't stay on your doorstep.'

Rosemary nudged the door open with an elbow and held it there.

'I won't come in now,' said Mrs Lionel. 'I'm running a few things up to Patti.' She held up the bundle of cloth she had in her arms. 'Tea towels. I've having a clean-up. I sorted out my linen cupboard and found I have far too many of nearly everything in there. Patti will turn them into a fancy tennis skirt or something else.' She smiled. 'Patti has an unusual but extraordinary talent for garment design.'

'Yes. She's an upcycling queen.'

Mrs Lionel lifted the tea towels in a gesture of farewell and continued up the pavement to Patricia's, Patti and Gerry's fashion house.

Rosemary stepped back from the door, letting it jangle closed. The heat from outside had crept in over the short time the door had been open. She heaved the boxy parcel up and took it to her living room, where a potted olive served as a Christmas tree. As she placed the parcel next to it, Sunny watched from her neat position on the couch. 'I don't think that one's for you, Sunny.'

I wouldn't want it anyway, the marmalade-coloured cat seemed to say as she stared unblinkingly at her mistress.

Rosemary stretched her back and glanced outside. The sky was deepening as the sun lowered, casting a velvety azure on the horizon. Venus shone brightly, fierce in the clear sky. *At this rate,* she thought, *Christmas Day will be one of the hottest on record.*

A knock at her door made her go back into the shop, wondering what Mrs Lionel had found now. Only it wasn't her best friend standing under the veranda: it was the team of firefighters.

Rosemary glanced over at the truck still stationary in the Square. 'Do you need help?'

'Yes,' said Clive, waving first at the fire truck and then at the town. 'We're stuck for the night. We can't get that thing started. It must have overheated like the rest of us.'

'It's old, like the rest of us,' said Claudia.

'Your mechanic has gone away for the Christmas break,' said Dennis. 'Too early, if you ask me.'

'No one asked you,' said Claudia. 'Mechanics needs holidays like the rest of us.'

'I'm not a mechanic,' Rosemary said.

'No, of course you aren't,' said Clive, peering around Rosemary to stare into the depths of The Preserved Mulbury. 'You are a cook.'

'Cooks could also be mechanics,' said Claudia. 'You shouldn't assume, Clive.'

'Clive? Assume?' Dennis gave a deep chuckle. 'Always been a bit quick to judge, eh, Clive?'

Rosemary held her hand up to stop the argument, which, she could tell from Clive's flushed face, was about to get worse. 'I am not a mechanic, and I'm not a cook. I'm an entrepreneur. That should cover all your concerns.'

It clearly didn't. Clive's mouth flapped without words coming out, Dennis looked blank, and Claudia mystified. 'Well,' Claudia said, pulling at the elastic of her uniform red trousers, 'it doesn't matter what you are. The problem is that we don't have transport and we need somewhere to stay.'

'And we're hoping you know of somewhere.' Dennis shrugged. 'Within walking distance.'

Rosemary studied the trio in front of her. Dennis and Clive were about the same height, but whereas Clive had the typically droopy arms of an older man, Dennis' arms were muscled, with thick forearms and prominent biceps bulging from his T-shirt sleeves. She could see the evidence of sunspots and patches on his skin. Definitely the signs of an outdoor worker.

Clive, on the other hand, looked soft. His jowls sagged and his neck had loose folds of skin. Nothing appeared to fit comfortably. He tugged his trousers up at regular intervals, tucking his shirt into the waistband in a vain attempt to keep it there.

Claudia was somewhere in between, as if she'd been an athlete once but hadn't exercised for quite a while. She stood slightly in front of the others, with her arms crossed over a heavy metal band T-shirt that might have been bought with someone else in mind. She had a sleeve of tattoos that which flashed as she put a hand up to smooth hair behind an ear. The three of them wore regulation red trousers and heavy black boots.

'It's after hours,' said Rosemary to the small expectant

crowd. 'And almost Christmas. Your chances of finding anywhere with a vacancy are small.'

'We'll have to sleep in the truck,' said Dennis, his mouth twisting at the thought.

'I'd rather lie out on the ground.' Claudia scowled at her colleagues. 'No offence, but it's hot and sticky and none of us smell very nice right now. And you snore.' She pointed to Clive. 'Or you do when you fall asleep when we're driving.'

Dennis laughed. 'Claudia's right. And you sniff a lot.'

'I get bad hay fever,' said Clive. 'You know that.'

'Sniffing and snoring...' Dennis poked Clive in the arm. 'It's like having an old dog in the cabin.'

Rosemary put her hand up. 'You have two choices. You make do in the truck or on the ground in the Square, or you can stay here. I've only got one spare bed, so you'll have to toss a coin who sleeps in it. After that, it's the couch or the carpet.'

'Well.' Claudia put her hands on her hips and smiled. 'That's very generous of you. I'll take you up. It's cooler in here than outside.'

'It is very nice,' said Clive, 'and much better for my bad back. Perhaps I could take the spare bed?'

'You can sort that out between you.' Rosemary pointed to the couch. 'This isn't bad either. I've spent a few nights on it myself.'

'Dennis can have the couch,' said Claudia. 'I'll take the floor.' She scowled at Clive. 'My back isn't so great, either, and it prefers a firm surface.'

'Done,' said Rosemary. 'Would you like dinner as well?'

The joyous look that passed over Clive's face said it for all of them. As Rosemary prepared a couscous salad to go with a range of cold meat and cheeses, Claudia and Dennis went back to the truck to lock it up and fetch their small number of belongings. Clive came to lean over the kitchen bench.

'So,' said Clive, when it was only the two of them, 'been here long?'

Rosemary flicked her long braid back over one shoulder and didn't look up from dicing semi-dried capsicum. 'Long enough to start this business and make a decent living.'

'Right.' Clive glanced back through the doorway to the adjoining shop. 'You sell jam.'

'Jams, jellies and pickles are my main stays.'

'Right.' Clive ran his finger along the bench top until he reached the chopping board and stole a small section of capsicum. 'Married, are you?'

Rosemary was saved from the indignation of a suitable rebuke by the loud jangling of the shop doorbell as Claudia, Dennis and another person came in. The fire fighters were arguing noisily about something and stormed into the living area, making Sunny flatten her ears and hiss. Behind them, his long black hair out of its man bun, came Jasper, looking as unhappy as the cat about the noise.

Rosemary put her knife down. 'Two things,' she said, in a strong clear voice that cut off the others. 'One. You are most welcome to stay, but the arguing must stop. The decibel range needs to stay below sixty-five or you can sleep in your truck. There are houses either side of the lounge room that share walls and your noise might wake Mrs Lionel or, less likely, Jasper.'

Jasper shrugged.

'Two. This house's cooling system relies on the thick brick outer walls keeping the sun out and a couple of ceiling fans. You need to change out of your heavy gear into something lighter or you will continue to perspire, and this room isn't big enough for the consequences arising from containing three sweaty people. Have you got any other suitable clothing?'

'We weren't expecting to be anywhere overnight,' said Dennis. 'I've only got what I'm wearing.'

'Same for all of us,' said Claudia. She held up a bag. 'We've really only got our handbags.'

'Man bag,' said Dennis, 'in my case.'

'I'll lend you some clothes,' said Rosemary. 'Jasper, have you got anything for the gentlemen?'

'I'll have a look.'

'Stay for dinner then.' Rosemary tilted her head to look at her friend. 'Unless you have other things planned.'

'Oh.' Jasper's face was the pleasing shade of red he went quite often in Rosemary's presence. 'Nothing planned. I'll be back shortly.'

Rosemary finished the salad and went to find Claudia a summery outfit. The fire fighter was as tall as Rosemary, but broader. Eventually, she found a blue dress that fell comfortably wide from the shoulders.

Claudia had followed Rosemary into her bedroom and took the outfit with a nod of thanks. She turned and whipped her black T-shirt off with a sigh of relief. 'I've been wearing that all day. I'm so glad to change.'

Claudia's back faced Rosemary. Even in the split second it took the fire fighter to slip the loose dress on, the scars stood out red and hard. Rosemary dropped her gaze, but Claudia saw her face as she turned back.

'It's okay,' she said, tugging the shirt down neatly. 'We all have them.'

'You all have burns.'

'Well,' Claudia ran her fingers through her greying hair to fluff it up. 'We were caught in the same blaze. A bushfire, way out in the country. We were out of the truck, planning our move. A tree fell. Took out all three of us. We were lucky to only get minor burns.' She shuddered. 'I hope I forget the feel of that searing heat landing on my back.'

Rosemary studied Claudia's face as something distressed flickered over it. *Perhaps*, she thought, *she'll never forget.* 'You said the tree took out three of you?'

'Yep. Three of us.' Claudia flung her arm towards the lounge room where the men waited for Jasper. 'Three of us got burned.' She stared straight at Rosemary. 'And Ivan didn't. That horrible man escaped without a mark.'

FOUR

Mrs Lionel lay down on her couch, curls settling among the embroidered cushions. Percy immediately hopped off his dog bed against the wall to lick her hand but, him not being alive, she couldn't feel it. 'Thank you, Percy,' she said to the smiling terrier. 'I'm alright. Just exhausted. I used to cope with the heat, but I'm not sure I do so well these days. Don't tell anyone.'

Percy gave an understanding yip and retreated to his bed, keeping an eye on his mistress like he was always destined to do.

From her place on the couch, and despite the whip whip of the ceiling fan set on high, Mrs Lionel could hear a low rumble of voices from Rosemary Exeter's adjoining living quarters. She'd seen two of the crew head to the fire truck and come back with a few bits and pieces and knew that they were staying on. *Rosemary can take care of herself,* she thought, but it was still a concern that someone had heated Ivan the fire volunteer to death, and that *someone* was likely to be at her friend's place right now.

A soft tapping on her shop door startled her. Mrs Lionel

glanced at her watch. It was later than she'd thought, well past dinnertime. *I must have fallen asleep,* she thought, and scrambled to sit. Once she'd got her bearings and patted her hair into place, she pushed herself upright and padded barefoot through the shop to see who was at the front door.

'Oh, Mrs Lionel, darling,' Rakisha said, as the electronic door frog croaked loudly. 'Really, darling, do you have to have that awful frog here? It disturbs my equilibrium every time.'

'I am sorry, Rakisha, but I do have to have him there to tell me whether customers have entered the shop. You get used to it. My equilibrium finds his noise quite a boost.'

Rakisha raked her flyaway hair out of her eyes and frowned. She was dressed, Mrs Lionel noted, in what appeared to be a long petticoat, although it was rimmed with purple velvet and the bodice had been fortified with denim. Rakisha saw the older woman's gaze and smiled. 'Oh, darling, you're looking at my Patricia's creation.'

'Patti made that for you?'

'I commissioned her.' Rakisha stroked the satin skirt. 'I had these favourite items of clothing, and she waved her magic wand to make me a summer dress. Isn't it divine, darling?'

Mrs Lionel leaned down to study the needlework more thoroughly. Patti Yale had a growing reputation for turning old or unloved garments into fashionable must-haves. Her design and sewing were truly genius. 'No magic wands here, Rakisha. Patti's work is exquisite.'

'Oh, she's an angel seamstress.' Rakisha bounced a bit on her leather sandals. 'Can I come in, Mrs Lionel, darling? I have something to show you.'

'Of course.' Mrs Lionel stepped back, letting the flouncing woman inside, and shut the door. The frog fell silent. 'Come into my lounge room and I'll get you a cold drink.'

'Marvellous, thank you. Have you any cranberry juice?'

'I do.' Mrs Lionel went to the fridge. 'Since you recommended it, I've always got some in the jug.'

'Oh, yes, darling, I told you it would help with your anti-oxidant levels and keep you youthful and vibrant.'

Mrs Lionel nodded, secretly wondering whether she'd better drink more. Cranberry juice was not really her taste, preferring a strong, hot cup of English breakfast tea even on a blistering day like that day had been. She poured them both a glass and handed Rakisha one. 'Now, you have something to show me?'

Rakisha let her oversized tote bag slip from her shoulder to the floor and bent over it. 'Yes, darling. Look.' She pulled a long, thin parcel out. It was wrapped in brown paper and finished with a jaunty red bow.

Mrs Lionel reached for it. 'A Christmas present.'

'It was hanging on the café doorknob as I opened it.'

'Ah.' Mrs Lionel plucked at the bow. 'I think we have a Kris Kringle among us.'

Rakisha put a hand to her throat. 'Is that bad, darling?'

'Not usually, dear. A Kris Kringle is like a secret Santa. Someone who gives you a gift at Christmas without you knowing who it came from.'

Rakisha's face screwed up. 'But, darling, what if I don't like the gift? Or the person giving it?'

Mrs Lionel felt her patience slip. 'It's a *gift*. You don't need to like it. It is the act of giving that shows the Christmas spirit. And you won't know who gave it to you. That's the point of it being secret.'

Rakisha drank her cranberry juice before nodding. 'Thank you, Mrs Lionel, darling. You always make things so much clearer for me.' She took the parcel back and shook it vigorously, making Mrs Lionel cringe. 'I wonder what it is.'

'You'll have to wait, dear. We open our presents on Christmas Day.'

'Then I will bring it along to Christmas lunch at Rosemary's.' Rakisha tucked the parcel back in her bag. 'Are you bringing anything?'

Mrs Lionel turned and pointed into the laundry where a plum pudding dangled in its unbleached bag looking like an over-sized Christmas tree bauble.

'Goodness, that doesn't look very tasty.'

Mrs Lionel tried not to frown. 'It will be delicious once served.'

'Lovely, then, darling Mrs Lionel.' Rakisha leaned forward. 'I'm making a pudding as well,' she whispered. 'Vegan. Ever so nice.'

Mrs Lionel pulled back a little as the other woman's long strands of hair tickled her face. 'Sounds wonderful, Rakisha. Your recipes are a constant source of surprise to me.'

Rakisha flicked her hair away and smiled. 'Do you know who else is coming to Christmas lunch, darling? One of them might be the Kris Kringle.'

'Jules and Roman have gone to their daughter's, and the Hubbard family is at the beach. Franco is thinking about it. Patti and Gerry will be there, as well as Jasper and Kelly.'

'Oh.' Rakisha slung the bag over her shoulder, catching wisps of hair and grimacing as she pulled them free. 'I do hope my Kris Kringle isn't Jasper.'

'Why on earth not?'

'Oh, darling, you know I don't read much. What good would a book be for me?'

Mrs Lionel clamped her lips shut. The parcel wasn't

remotely book-shaped, and despite owning a successful bookshop, Jasper Lu could think of other things as a present.

'I'd better go, darling. I am preparing my special iced chilli herbal tea for tomorrow's customers.'

'Chilli?'

'Oh yes, darling. Chilli lowers the temperature of the blood. Goodness, I thought everyone knew that.' She brushed more hair away. 'Bye for now, darling Mrs Lionel.'

Rakisha wove her way out of Mrs Lionel's living room, through the shop and opened the door, jumping sideways as the frog croaked a farewell. Mrs Lionel followed and closed the door after her, fanning herself with her hand as a blast of warm air from outside rolled in. Through the dimness of the evening, she saw Rakisha had made it safely across Goldmarket Road and to The Sweet Potato where she lived above her shop.

Despite the temperature outside being well above comfortable, Mrs Lionel took her dinner outside to eat on the porch that overlooked the back garden. Each of the four shops under the one veranda at the front also had porches stretching out from their backs, with wooden steps that led down to long backyards that ended at the creek. Mrs Lionel had let her yard grow wild, and it was a jumble of herbs and perennials. Next door, Rosemary's was much more organised, with vegetable patches and fruit trees. She also had chickens and ducks, now locked up for the night against marauding foxes, that supplied many residents with fresh eggs. Jasper's yard was mainly dirt at this time of the year, with one or two large gum trees shading some berry canes. Patti and Gerry's was paved with red bricks. Being in the house next to the road to Big Town, Gerry kept their car in the yard.

'Mrs Lionel,' called a voice from over the rail. 'Would you like to join us for dinner?'

Mrs Lionel showed her empty plate to Rosemary. 'I thought I'd sit out here for a change, although it isn't any cooler.'

'No.' Rosemary glanced back inside her house. 'But it's a good idea. I've got three extras tonight, and it's heating the place up.'

'That was good of you, dear, to take them in.'

Rosemary said nothing.

Mrs Lionel grinned. 'It wasn't anything to do with being good, was it? You have them all under suspicion.'

'I didn't say that.'

'Rosemary Exeter, you rarely have to say anything for me to know what's going on in your head. How are they?'

'They grumble a lot.'

'At you?'

'No. At each other.' Rosemary straightened. 'Jasper's here, helping me keep the peace, not that he's very good at solving conflicts. Could I entice you over for dessert? Nothing spectacular. Bottled pears and ice-cream.'

'Sounds delicious. I'll be over in fifteen minutes.'

Rosemary went back inside to the noise of three people arguing over something. The noise stopped as she entered, and Mrs Lionel smiled again. One narrow-eyed look from Rosemary would stop most bickering in its tracks. After fifteen minutes, she rose, took her plate inside, nodded to Percy, and went next door.

Clive was gathering dirty plates together as Mrs Lionel entered the room. He was concentrating so hard on carrying them to the kitchen that he didn't notice the older woman at the doorway. He startled, and cutlery slid noisily to the floor, making Claudia jump, Dennis shudder and Jasper smile.

'I'm sorry, dear. I didn't mean to scare you.'

'Oh no, not at all.' Clive tried to juggle the pile of plates in either hand and gave up as Jasper bent to retrieve the knives and forks. 'I mean, you aren't scary at all.'

'Oh,' said Mrs Lionel with a glance at Rosemary, 'I can be.'

Clive looked even more startled.

'Mrs Lionel,' said Rosemary. 'Come and sit here.'

Mrs Lionel sat next to Rosemary on one side of the table, which gave her a great view of the three fire volunteers. As Clive slid back into his seat, she noted the strange array of clothing they wore: a T-shirt strained across Dennis's stomach that read "Don't talk to me, I'm reading", the polo shirt on Clive had an imprint of a famous London bookshop on its pocket, and a loose blue tunic on Claudia showed a long line of tattoos on one arm. None of them were happy, despite the large bowls of ice-cream Jasper was now placing in front of them. 'You must be very sad, dears, about your friend Ivan.'

'Colleague,' said Claudia at the same time as Dennis said 'Teammate' and Clive muttered 'Co-worker'.

'I see,' said Mrs Lionel.

'We're very sad, though,' said Claudia. 'Aren't we?'

The others nodded.

Mrs Lionel ate her ice-cream saying nothing else, but nudged Rosemary's knee under the table. Rosemary tipped her head slightly towards the coat rack standing at the sliding doors to Rosemary's porch. From under the waterproof coat Rosemary wore when gardening in the rain, the edge of the Santa suit poked out, a dull red in the shadows. When it was Rosemary's turn to gather the dishes, she bent down briefly to Mrs Lionel's ear. 'Can you take it? I'll pass it over the porch rail later.'

'Yes.' Mrs Lionel handed her a spoon. 'Do you have any evidence of wrongdoing?'

'Nothing definite. I need your expertise.'

There wasn't a chance to say more. Mrs Lionel sat thinking about her areas of expertise. Was it her knowledge of green cleaning products Rosemary wanted? Or the fact that she'd been a nurse and then a dairy farmer? Maybe it was because she'd been around longer than anyone on Goldmarket Road.

With Rosemary's mind working on a dozen theories, who would know?

FIVE

The heat hadn't deterred last minute Christmas Eve shoppers, or maybe the early opening hours had made the heat bearable. A minibus pulled up in the street the next day right on seven o'clock and disgorged a group of tourists already wearing floppy hats and sunglasses. Some went straight for Kelly's Mullings of Mulbury, emerging minutes later with large, iced coffees. The one or two that had ventured into The Sweet Potato also clutched cold drinks, although the looks on their faces were bemused as they sipped their fiery purchases. A couple wandered over to the fire truck, pausing to look around as if expecting a fire nearby, but soon made their way to the shops under the veranda on Goldmarket Road.

Rosemary propped the door of The Preserved Mulbury open while the early hour allowed a semblance of cool air. Mulbury Mornings had worked for two reasons: enticing those early tourists but also allowing the residents of Mulbury to get their final Christmas purchases. Clive and Claudia fell into the first category. They rose with the sun and disappeared outside to explore the town. 'Would you like some breakfast first?' said Rosemary as they prepared to leave.

Claudia had glanced at the couch where Dennis was snoring noisily. 'No. But thanks. I've got to get away from that.'

Rosemary watched from her shop counter, noticing that Claudia turned left to The Green Mulbury while Clive marched straight across the road toward the fire truck.

Gerry wandered in not long after wearing an interesting brown velour smoking jacket, which he pulled closed across his belly several times during his selection of five jars of lemon marmalade and three of pear chutney. 'I forgot,' he said to Rosemary as he tightened the cord once again across his middle. 'We have to visit Patti's sisters on Boxing Day. I was meant to get them something more Christmassy.'

Rosemary packed the last jar into a paper carry bag. 'What could be more Christmassy than preserves?'

Gerry laughed. 'I'm with you on that. But I think the presents were meant to be more personal. You know, perfume for Rachel and a tennis racquet for Delia.'

'Marmalade and chutney are much more practical for women who could buy their own perfume and sports gear.'

'I said to Patti she should make garments for them.' Gerry shook his head. 'Those women don't realise what a genius they have for a sister.'

Rosemary could only agree. 'Is Patti busy today?'

Gerry shook his head. 'Not particularly. All her orders were picked up yesterday, so we'll only have spontaneous trade this morning.'

'Tell her I've got a favour to ask.'

Gerry's eyebrows shot up. 'Oh?'

'I'll be down to see her later this morning.'

Gerry waited, but Rosemary said nothing more. After

raising his bag in farewell, Gerry wandered back to Patricia's to dress before the real customers noticed he remained in his sleeping attire.

Dennis was late to rise. Rosemary kept the door to her living area closed as she served the minibus occupants, but even their chatter didn't disturb him. Rosemary slipped back into her kitchen for a drink and finally Dennis poked his head above the couch. 'Ah,' he said, 'morning already?'

'Christmas Eve.'

He nodded and rubbed his eyes. 'I was so tired last night. I slept like a log.' He peered around the room. 'Where are the others?'

'They went shopping.'

'Oh.' Dennis struggled up. 'What are they shopping for?'

'Breakfast. Christmas presents. They would be my best guesses.'

'Did they say anything about the truck?'

'I haven't seen them since.'

Dennis opened his phone and peered closely at it. 'There's nothing about it on my phone. Or not that I can see. Where did I put my glasses?'

'Here.' Rosemary crouched and picked up a pair of spectacles from the floor. 'They must have fallen down.'

Dennis reached for them and looked at his phone again. 'I've still got that morning blur, but there's no message here yet from the mechanic. Looks like we're stuck in Mulbury for a while longer. I'm going to explore the sights while I can.'

'Everything's open,' said Rosemary. 'If you want to see the sights of the old town, though, you'll need to get going before it gets too hot.'

'That's right,' said Dennis, gazing out the back window. 'Don't want to get too hot.' He chuckled to himself.

Rosemary frowned.

As Dennis got ready for the day, Rosemary went back to the shop to serve the early birds. She kept half an ear open on the activity inside her home, but only heard yawns and coughs as Dennis moved slowly around the lounge room. Eventually, he emerged dressed in a combination of red uniform trousers and Jasper's shirt, looking tousled and weary.

She waited until he'd jangled out the door and gone to join Clive, who was still inspecting the truck before ducking out to The Green Mulbury, pulling her jangling door shut behind her. Mrs Lionel was serving an older couple, and Rosemary loitered near some dried oregano until the customers left before approaching the shop counter. 'Cup of tea, dear?' said Mrs Lionel.

'No time now. Did you look at the jacket I put over the rail?'

Mrs Lionel nodded. 'Standard issue Santa suit with a little surprise sewn in.'

'The heated vest.'

'Yes. And it was still on, so the batteries weren't flat. It would be very snuggly on a chilly day.'

'Very, *very* snuggly on a hot day.'

'Yes.' Mrs Lionel shook her head. 'Overheating of the body's core would occur quite quickly on a day like yesterday.' She glanced outside at the searingly blue sky. 'And today.'

'I'm going to take the jacket to Patti. She'll be able to tell us more about how the vest was fastened to the material.'

'Excellent idea, Rosemary Exeter. I'll watch the shops while you're gone.'

'Where is the jacket?'

'On the back of my armchair.' Mrs Lionel watched as Rosemary went to get it. 'Put it in a bag, dear. The fire team are milling around the Square and they might see you.'

Rosemary folded the heavy jacket into a bag, feeling how the material still felt warm, and left Mrs Lionel's shop with a nod. As she walked along the pavement to Patricia's, she could see Dennis and Clive looking at the truck's engine. Clive nodded jerkily at her as he ran a hand through his thinning hair, and she tipped her head to show she'd seen him.

Patti Yale stood outside her shop fussing with a rack of dresses that Rosemary assumed by their heavy brocade had been made from curtains. 'Oh, Rosemary.' Patti wafted a large paper fan. 'It's so hot already. What a good idea of yours to have our shops open early. I've already sold a few garments.'

'From those on the minibus?'

'Oh, yes, sweetie. Christmas presents for their grandchildren, you know. Lots of lost sock puppets and upcycled hats.'

'Right.' Rosemary glanced at the window display Patti was pointing at that featured a colourful array of socks and hats decorated with lace and buttons and accompanied by a copious amount of tinsel. 'Do you have a moment to look at something for me?'

Patti put one hand to a rosy cheek and rocked to the toes of her ballet flats and back to their heels, making her 1950s floral dress sway. The apricot-coloured hair curled at her neck, held loosely by a yellow headband, oscillated with her, and Rosemary had to blink to stop herself thinking they might have tripped back in time to a former era. 'Yes, Rosemary, of course. Should we go inside?'

'Yes.'

Patti led the way, opening the squealing front door of the shop and leaping over the step to its interior. Rosemary followed, threading her way through mannikins dressed in smartly patched suits and slim skirts. Gerry glanced up from his perch at the shop counter and smiled. 'Rosemary. Tea?'

'Of course.'

As Gerry disappeared into the kitchen to do what he did best, Rosemary pulled the Santa jacket from her bag.

'What is that, Rosemary?' Patti stretched her hand out, then paused. 'Oh. That's the suit the poor man was wearing yesterday.'

'Yes. Take it. See what you think.'

'I don't-' Patti nearly dropped the jacket as it was handed to her. 'It's so heavy. They usually make Santa suits from a light polyester. I know because I turned one into a playsuit after last Christmas.' She turned the lapels back to look inside. 'What on earth is that?'

'A heated vest, Patti. It was sewn inside.'

'Whatever for? It's not like an Australian Santa has to plough through the snow to get to any house around here.'

'Exactly.'

Patti put the jacket on the sewing bench behind the counter and opened its arms to expose the inside. She sat down and flicked on a reading lamp to peer more closely at the stitching. 'Tell me more.'

'It appears that Santa was overheated. Deliberately.'

'Goodness.' Patti ran her finger down the edge of the vest. 'Someone put this in for Santa to wear and it *killed* him?'

'That may not have been the intention.'

'But it happened anyhow. Gosh.' Patti's finger stopped. 'This is interesting.'

Rosemary leaned over the woman's shoulder, holding her braid back to stop it dangling in the way. 'What is it?'

'Well.' Patti shifted back a little so Rosemary could see. 'The vest is made from heavy nylon material and would need strong thread to sew it firmly to anything else. When worn, the vest took all the weight, so the rest of the jacket was really acting as a cover. This thread, though, is unusual for a garment.'

'What do you mean?'

'Since I used the last of my silk embroidery threads, I've done a lot of recent research into threads of all kinds.' Patti sighed. 'I do so miss my threads, especially as they came from a house lot of sewing items dumped on a nature strip. But this is not something you'd normally buy from a haberdasher. I'd say it's come from a camping or sporting store.'

'So, the person who sewed it may have been versed in camping?'

'Or knew to take it to a store that normally sewed canvas or other heavy materials. It's very neatly done so likely to be a professional using a decent sewing machine.' Patti leaned back. 'I bet they wondered why they were sewing a heated vest into a Santa suit.'

'Yes.' Rosemary lifted the collar of the vest from the table. 'No clothing label.'

'In the garments I find abandoned like lost souls on the side of the road, about half have no labels.' Patti shrugged. 'Labels can be itchy things.'

'People cut them off. This vest wasn't new, then.'

'Oh no. It's quite worn on the inside. You can tell by the shininess of the parts that have rested on someone's torso.'

Rosemary ran her hand down the inside of the vest,

feeling the change from rough to smooth, imagining how the vest had rested on its original owner. 'Anything else, Patti?'

'Clues, do you mean?' Patti shook her head, her waves swinging. 'The only other thing I can notice is that the vest was sewn on recently. The thread is new. I'd say it was in preparation for this Christmas season.'

Rosemary stepped back as Patti stood. Two customers had entered the shop, and the seamstress smiled apologetically to Rosemary as she skipped toward them. Rosemary took her place at the table and pulled the lamp down to look more closely at the thread. It was black and sturdy, definitely not the type Patti would use for her bespoke creations. She folded the jacket up to put back in the bag, lifting it up in farewell to Patti, and left the shop.

It was roasting outside. Magpies stood in miserable groups underneath The Exceptional Tree, wings lifted from their bodies. Franco had placed a baking tray of water there for them, and the birds took it in turn to sit in and bathe. As Rosemary crossed Goldmarket Road to the Square, she saw some of Mulbury's visitors gazing longingly at the dish as if wishing it was an Olympic-sized swimming pool.

'Hello, Rosemary,' Clive said as she approached the fire truck. 'Been shopping?'

'No.'

Clive waited for her to say more, but when she said nothing, he eased himself upright from his position leaning on the truck and raised his phone. 'Vijay, the mechanic, is on his way from Big Town. Dennis thinks he has correctly identified the problem and that it will take an hour or two to fix.'

'Yep,' said Dennis, wiping a forearm across his brow. 'We should be home in time for an evening fish.'

'You're a fisherman,' said Rosemary.

'Angler, please.' Dennis grinned. 'It's what I'm going to do all day long once I retire.'

'Good luck with that,' said Claudia, hands on hips. 'We haven't got a lot of waterways around here.'

'I go to the reservoir.'

'Nice,' said Clive. 'I go camping there. It's very peaceful.'

'You don't fish, though, eh?' said Dennis. 'You go to lounge about in a camping chair, and stare at the sky.'

'I'm a twitcher,' said Clive to Rosemary. 'A bird watcher.'

'Right.'

'Couldn't think of anything more boring,' said Claudia.

'Oh, yeah?' Clive frowned at his colleague. 'I could. *Hiking.*'

'At least hiking gets you active.' Claudia looked pointedly at Clive's soft stomach.

Clive patted his abdomen. 'It's been worse.'

Before they could launch into a heated discussion about the merits of their various pastimes, Rosemary raised her hand. 'Got it,' she said. 'A fisher person, a twitcher, and a hiker. All very outdoor orientated.'

'That we are,' said Dennis. 'That's the one thing we have in common.' He slapped a hand on his leg. 'I say we go get a cold drink and sit inside until the mechanic arrives.'

'Best idea you've ever had.' Clive pointed at Kelly's. 'I say that one. I've seen lots of cream-topped ice coffees come out of there.' He turned to Rosemary. 'Would you like one?'

'No. Thank you. I'll get back to work.'

'Righto, then.'

Rosemary watched as the fire volunteers walked across the Square to the café. Voluntary fire officers, whose day jobs were a builder, a dairy worker and a meat inspector, and who liked to fish, birdwatch and hike. All of which would, at some stage of the year, feature inhospitable environments. Occupations and hobbies that would benefit from a heated vest.

And, she thought, as she crossed the road back to The Preserved Mulbury, all three had reasons to dislike Ivan.

SIX

Kelly Flanagan heard the door of the café creak open and frowned. Only hours until she shut for Christmas, and people were still barrelling in for drinks and jelly slices. She was halfway through packing yo-yos in boxes to give as presents to her uncles, reminiscing about past Christmas baking experiences, and she had to pause yet again. She braced herself and clamped a smile on her face. 'Hello,' she said as brightly as she could conjure. 'Looking for a cool drink?'

'My word,' said one of the three fire volunteers clustered in front of the counter. 'It's hot enough to roast a pig out there.'

Kelly studied the trio's red trousers and tried not to think of roasted pig. She had heard the news, as everyone in Mulbury had, that their companion had died of heat exhaustion. *Roasted fire fighter,* she thought, and felt her lip curl. 'Roast pork might be what's happening tomorrow,' she said. 'Or is it roast turkey at your place?'

'Come on, Dennis,' said the woman. 'What are you cooking for Christmas lunch?'

'I don't cook, Claudia, as you well know. I'm going to my sister's.' Dennis closed his eyes and smiled. 'She'll have the usual array of ham and turkey, crisp potatoes and pumpkin, with enough greens to feed an army of guinea pigs.' He opened his eyes. 'Then we'll have a selection of plum pudding, pavlova, trifle and chocolate ripple cake.'

'Oh, stop it,' said the other man. 'You're making me hungry.'

'What goes down for your Christmas lunch, Clive?' Claudia stooped to look at Kelly's display of cakes.

'This year, the family's coming to our house so it's cold meats and salads.' Clive sighed. 'Ivan was going to come as well. Kath felt sorry for him.'

'Well, you won't have to worry about him spoiling things.' Claudia paused to read the label of an extravagantly iced sponge. 'But what will you be eating?'

'I wanted to have seafood, but Kath said no. She's worried that we're too far from the sea to get fresh produce.'

'That's a load of rubbish,' Dennis said. 'Big Town gets seafood within a day or two of it being caught. It comes straight from the fish market in the city.'

'You try to convince Kath of that.'

'There'll be something good for dessert, though.' Claudia moved along the cake display to take in the rest of it. 'Ice cream pudding or mince tarts or something.'

'Nope.' Clive's mouth turned down. 'Even on Christmas Day, Kath likes to keep things trim. She'll have a lovely fruit salad for us. With yoghurt.'

'Well,' said Kelly, 'I'm sure it will all be delicious. Now. What can I do for you today?'

'We haven't heard what you're having, Claudia?' said Dennis, squinting at the menu board behind Kelly's head. 'It's usually something much more exotic.'

'I'm not sure you would call paella exotic, Dennis. It's more a family tradition. It's always too hot for roast meat, and cold meat and salad are what we have most of the summer anyhow. So, we decided to change things up. Paella does that.'

'Fantastic,' Kelly said, sounding decidedly unimpressed. 'Now. Today?'

'I tell you what you could do, Clive.' Dennis tapped the glass cabinet. 'Buy a whole heap of these yummy looking cakes for tomorrow. You can say you were helping out...' He waved his hand at Kelly.

'Kelly.'

'Kelly here.' He looked around at the neat shop with its white walls decorated with colourful paintings of famous gold nuggets. The Welcome Stranger took pride of place in the middle. 'I'm sure Kelly would appreciate it.'

Kelly wasn't convinced she was going to appreciate it. The sudden glint in Clive's eye made her wonder if he wasn't about to buy the lot, including the carefully packed yo-yos.

Clive, however, must have felt the wrath of Kath bearing down on him. 'Grand idea, Dennis, but I might have a chocolate chip biscuit for now. Oh, make it two. One for now, one later. What about coffee, everyone? My shout.'

'Really?' said Claudia. 'The only shout I've ever heard you make is *don't drive so fast!*'

'Oh, ha ha, Claudia.' Clive frowned, his eyes almost disappearing behind his drawn eyebrows. 'It's Christmas Eve, for goodness' sake. Just order a coffee.'

After they placed coffee orders, the trio sat at an inside table directly under the air-conditioner while Kelly set the coffee machine going. The man called Clive angled his chair so he could see the outside world and the inside of the shop, while Dennis sat right up at the table like a boy waiting for his dinner. Claudia pushed her chair back a little, stretching her arms out above her head, displaying the intricate tattoos on her arms. One caught Kelly's eye: a little dog, eyes bright and stubby tail up. It reminded her of Pudge, the dog she grew up with. *I was only talking about him the other day,* she thought as the machine hissed. *Now who was that to...?*

'Alright then, Kelly?' Clive smiled at her.

'Yes. Won't be a moment.'

He gave a little wave.

She made another coffee, keeping an eye on him as she worked. He sat easily in his chair, glancing at the truck now and then as if waiting for something, yawning and stretching like a lazy cat. *Like that cat of Rosemary Exeter's,* Kelly thought. *Sunshine, or whatever it's called.*

Thinking of Rosemary Exeter, as unpleasant as that was, made Kelly remember the fire volunteers had stayed there overnight. They must have been too distressed about what had happened to their friend. She carried their drinks over to them on a tray and sat it on their table. 'Bad luck, what happened yesterday.'

'Oh, they'll come and fix it,' said Dennis, taking his cup and stirring a spoon of sugar into it.

Kelly stopped halfway through delivering Clive's biscuit. 'I beg your pardon?'

Clive took the plate from her. 'The mechanic is on his way.'

'I meant, about your friend.'

'Friend?' Dennis stared at her for a moment. 'Oh. You mean what happened to Ivan.'

'Oh that,' said Clive.

'Yes,' said Kelly. 'That. It must have been awful.'

A moment passed before all three heads started nodding and there were mutters of 'Awful. Terrible. Sad.'

Kelly stood back and put her hands on her hips. 'And you stayed with Rosemary.'

'Because of the broken-down truck,' said Claudia. 'By the time we mucked around with it and realised it would not start, it was late. Rosemary let us stay.'

'How kind of her.'

'Yes, very kind.' Clive took a huge bite of his biscuit. 'Nice woman, Rosemary.'

Kelly grimaced. 'I find her cold.'

'Cold?' Clive shook his head. 'A little aloof perhaps.'

'Practical,' said Claudia.

'Straight-forward,' said Dennis, sipping his coffee.

'Cold.' Kelly thought back to Alasdair, Rosemary's husband, and his handsome figure, which had been totally wasted on a cold fish like the owner of The Preserved Mulbury. 'She drives people away.'

The fire volunteers turned perplexed eyes toward her, but she was saved from explaining how the gorgeous Alasdair had gone by the loud ringing of Clive's phone. 'Ah,' he said as he answered it, 'the mechanic.'

'Here, is he?' asked Claudia.

'He made a detour into the bookshop, so he'll be a few minutes.'

Dennis craned his neck to see out the window. 'There's his truck. Jeepers.'

'What?' Clive half-stood to have a look as well, clutching his trouser top as he did to stop his pants from sliding down. 'Are they reindeer's antlers?'

'Yes,' said Claudia, shaking her head. 'You buy them at

the variety stores and put one antler on either side of your car.'

'Well,' said Clive, sitting back down with a thump. 'I've never seen them before.'

'All the rage in the city.' Dennis pushed his chair back and stood up. 'Come on. Let's get him out of the bookshop and working on our truck. I would like to get home some time today.'

'Thank you for the coffees,' said Clive to Kelly as he followed suit.

Kelly watched as Clive picked up his two biscuits and tried to push them into his top pocket. 'Would you like a bag for those?'

'Yeah, Clive,' said Dennis. 'Kath will see the crumbs in your pocket and guess what you've been up to.'

Claudia laughed. 'Then it'll be lettuce leaves for Christmas lunch.'

Clive pulled the biscuits back out roughly, leaving a scattering of crumbs on his front and on the floor of the café. Kelly produced a paper bag, and he took a bite out of one biscuit before dropping the rest into it. 'Delicious,' he said, spitting a few more crumbs into the air.

'I'll get the door for you,' said Kelly, skirting around the mess and beating them to it. As she opened it, hot air billowed toward her as if it had been waiting impatiently to come inside.

'Thank you,' said Claudia as she stepped out. 'I apologise for the behaviour of my starved colleague.'

Kelly slapped on another smile as her customers exited, but let it drop the moment she shut the door behind them. She went to the storeroom to get a broom, dodging the curing Christmas pudding hanging from a hook in the roof, and returning to find that crumbs weren't the only mess they'd left behind. They'd also tracked in stones and dirt caught in their working boots from the surface of Gold-market Square. *Honestly,* she thought as she swept vigor-ously, *these are the people that Mulbury doesn't need.*

She'd just pushed the mess into a neat pile when someone opened the door, making the pile skitter over the floor again.

'Sorry, love,' said Clive, pushing the door shut behind him. 'I've had another thought, based on the delicious nature of your biscuits. Could I have a selection of your goodies?'

Kelly left the dirt and went behind the counter. 'What would you like?' she said tightly.

'Let me think.' He lifted his hand to rest it on the glass display, making a brown package bang against it. 'Oh. This was hanging on your doorknob.'

'Really?' Kelly took the parcel from him. 'What is it?'

'Oh, goodness, I don't know.'

Kelly put the package down, somewhat awkwardly, as it was a strange shape. It was tied with a curl of shiny green. 'Well,' she said. 'That'll be something interesting to open Christmas Day. Now. A morsel for you to eat?'

Clive took his time to choose, umming and ahhing between the lemon tarts and apple cakes. Kelly drummed her fingers on the bench, unable to do anything else but study the man in front of her. He had neat, grey hair and a clean-shaved neck that was evident as he leaned sideways to check how thick the layer of meringue was on its lemon base. She glimpsed the chain of a silver necklace under the collar of a shirt that was too large for Clive and quite famil-iar. *Jasper Lu's?* she wondered. *Was he at Rosemary's last night as well?* She bristled. Rosemary Exeter had certainly landed on her feet after Alasdair, confirming Kelly's opinion that the woman was too cunning beyond that cool exterior.

'-sugar?'

Kelly blinked. Clive stared at her, a questioning arch to one eyebrow.

'I'm sorry, say again?'

'I'm looking for the one with the least amount of sugar.' Clive pointed to the cabinet. 'I really shouldn't be having any.'

Kelly closed her eyes briefly. 'Well,' she said slowly, 'they are cakes. And tarts. All of them have decent amounts of sugar. That's what makes them so delicious. If you don't want an item with sugar, you could go to The Sweet Potato. Rakisha thinks sugar is the enemy of the free world.'

'Oh.' Clive shook his head. 'That sounds terrible. No, I need some, but not the worst one.' He gazed at her with that same imploring eyebrow action.

'Take these.' Kelly scooped a square of hazelnut slice and a slice of pecan tart into a cardboard tray. 'The nuts balance the sugar.'

'Really?' Clive grinned. 'I must remember that for the future.'

'How about I keep them here in the cool until your truck is fixed?' She slid the tray back into the display cabinet. 'They'll melt in the heat.'

He nodded solemnly. 'Thank you for understanding a sad old man's whims.'

Kelly frowned. 'Sad?'

'Perhaps not as much as I was.' Clive's smile widened. 'And away from my darling wife, I'm entitled to a treat now and then.'

'Everyone is entitled to eat a cake or two, especially at Christmas time.'

Clive nodded. 'Yes indeed. But I also like to treat myself in other ways.' He leaned over and tapped the side of his nose. 'If you get my drift.'

For a split second, Kelly puzzled over his comment, but the moment he opened the door to leave, letting more hot air scatter the pile of debris further over the shop floor, his drift had completely disappeared out of her head.

SEVEN

Mrs Lionel turned the ceiling fan in The Green Mulbury to its highest setting, stirring the "Clean Green" leaflets from her counter and making the racks of drying herbs along the back wall rock. She'd chocked the connecting door open to let more air circulate. Extra air wasn't usually needed amongst the packages of soap and tea towels on her shelves as the solid, outer, double-layer of bricks of the walls and the expansive veranda normally kept the heat out of all the shops along Goldmarket Road. 'Too much for too long,' she said to Percy as he stood watching her, his tail whipping from side to side. 'If you had a pulse, you'd be feeling it, too.'

Percy's tongue lolled as he panted happily. Not for the first time, Mrs Lionel was glad the terrier had stayed on, albeit in a ghostly state, when he'd died.

The croaking of the electronic frog heralded a visitor, and Mrs Lionel turned to greet them as Percy disappeared through the house doorway. 'Oh, it's you, Rosemary, dear.'

'Yes.' Rosemary pushed the door shut with one foot and stepped away from the frog to shut it up. 'I brought you cold barley water.'

'Barley water? I haven't had that for decades.'

'Then you'll appreciate it.' Rosemary handed her friend a glass. 'You need to keep up your fluids on a day like today.'

'As do you.' Mrs Lionel sipped the cloudy water. 'Lovely. Refreshing, isn't it? Quite the drink for today, although you can't beat-'

'-a cup of tea.' Rosemary smiled. 'I know. You can have your tea as well, then you'll get twice the fluids.'

'Clever you.' Mrs Lionel perched on the stool behind the counter. 'How did you get on with Patti?'

'The heated vest was sewn in with a strong thread used by businesses that mend outdoor equipment. Most likely not by a seamstress.'

'That would make sense. The material is quite thick.'

'Yes. Patti also noticed wear patterns on the vest, so it wasn't new by any means.'

'I see.' Mrs Lionel sipped her drink. 'I am wondering, dear, whether the jacket was part of their original Santa suit, or did it come from elsewhere? The fire brigade does a lot of community work around Christmas time. It's not unusual to see a Santa on the back of a fire truck in country towns all over the state. It might help to know where the suit came from.'

'Good point.' Rosemary bent to sniff the array of hand-made soaps displayed in trays next to the counter, nodding appreciatively. 'I assumed the suit belonged to that particular fire brigade. What if it was given to Ivan to wear by someone else?'

'You need to ask them.'

'Yes.' Rosemary reached for Mrs Lionel's glass. 'Finished? I'll take it back.'

'Leave the glasses here and I'll wash them first.' Mrs Lionel took Rosemary's. 'You go question our suspects.'

Rosemary left Mrs Lionel fanning herself with a spray of dried thyme and ventured back into the heat. The day was becoming dull as high cloud covered the bold blue sky, and the wind blew in foul gusts across the Square as she crossed it. The fire volunteers stood in a group around the truck's bonnet, watching a man in green overalls bang something with a spanner, but Rosemary saw how alert they were to the conditions. Clive even licked his finger and held it up to the wind.

'A northerly,' said Rosemary as she approached them.

Clive glanced at her and nodded. 'My word, Rosemary, you are a surprise.'

'I am?'

'You knew exactly what I was doing.' He punched his finger up again, making Rosemary pull back. 'Testing the weather.'

'This is the other way to do it.' Claudia held up her phone. 'Everything's at your fingertips. Wind speed, direction, force. I can tell you everything you want to know.'

'Perhaps.' Clive shrugged. 'Looking at a screen doesn't help me with honing my instincts.' He closed his eyes and raised his chin to sniff the air. 'No rain coming, and this wind is a worry. If it keeps up, I wouldn't want to see a fire start. We'd have trouble stopping it.'

Claudia studied her screen. 'This says it's going to be alright. The wind will swing around later this afternoon, and the temperature will drop.'

'Ah,' said Clive, 'but will it be in time?'

'Heavens, Clive,' said Dennis. 'We've got enough trouble getting this truck going. If a fire comes hooking over the hill, we're not going to be of much use.' He tipped his head toward the man leaning over the truck bonnet. 'Vijay's got to go back to Big Town to get a part.'

'So, we're stuck here for longer?'

'We don't all have to stay,' said Claudia. 'By the time the truck's fixed, we won't have time to do any more Santa gigs today. Only one of us has to drive the truck back.'

'We might have time to do a gig here.' Dennis turned to Rosemary. 'What do you think? We could set up in the Square and entertain the visitors.'

'It's up to you,' said Rosemary. 'Although, you're missing one vital ingredient.'

'Really?' Dennis looked around him as if that ingredient might be in the air. 'What?'

'You don't have a Santa.'

Dennis hesitated. In that moment, Rosemary took in the faces of the three fire volunteers. Claudia's face was blank, as if she hadn't heard the statement properly. Dennis's mouth had fallen open slightly. Clive rubbed his cheek hard, scratching through his stubble pensively.

'We don't need Ivan to have a Santa,' said Claudia at last. 'All of us have been Santa at some stage. I played Santa last year on this very truck.' She pointed to Dennis. 'You told me you were Santa for your work break up this Christmas.'

Dennis shuffled his feet, raising dust from the gravelly surface of the Square. 'That's right. I dressed up for the crew. Even arrived in the back of a work truck, ringing a bell and yelling "Ho, ho, ho".' He shook his head. 'Haven't lived it down since.'

'Oh, they would have secretly loved it.' Clive slapped Dennis's back. 'You're such a jolly fellow.'

'Jolly shmolly.' Dennis grinned suddenly. 'You were Santa a few years ago. Turned up at the abattoir in the town where I was building a hall. All I remember was your very red face.'

'Takes a lot of effort, giving out presents,' said Clive.

'You've had the experience before,' said Rosemary. 'All you need is the suit.'

Dennis frowned. 'I can't remember exactly what happened. Wasn't Ivan still dressed in the suit when they...'

'Took him to hospital,' finished Clive. 'They will have thrown it out by now.'

'He wasn't dressed in an entire Santa suit,' said Dennis, pulling at the legs of his trousers. 'He had his usual uniform on his bottom half.'

'The suit was only a jacket, a beard and a hat.' Claudia flicked her thumb towards the truck. 'They're in there.'

'You sure?' said Dennis. 'I didn't put them in there.'

'I think so.' Claudia opened the back door of the cabin and leaned in. 'Something's stuffed behind the seat, and the hat and beard are on the floor.'

As she was searching, the mechanic closed the bonnet and stood back to wipe his hands on his overalls. 'Right, I'll be back,' he said. 'Anyone for a ride to Big Town?'

'Got it.' Claudia backed out of the cabin with a bundle of red clothing. She unfurled two things. 'See? Padded suit jacket, Santa's beard and hat.'

Indeed, thought Rosemary as she stared at the red clothes rocking in the rough breeze. A fur-trimmed Santa jacket, a matted beard, and a red V-shaped hat. *But not the jacket that Ivan had been wearing.*

'Hey,' said Vijay impatiently. 'Last offer. Anyone coming back with me?'

'Ah,' said Clive, 'no. I think I'll stay. Kath will only have me cleaning up ready for tomorrow. I don't fancy de-cobwebbing the eaves on a day like today.'

'I'll stay, as well.' Dennis took the jacket from Claudia, studying it closely. 'Everything's under control at home.'

'Well, if you two are staying, then I will, too.' Claudia looked at Vijay. 'Maybe we'll be able to do some fundraising yet. Thanks for the offer. You won't be long, though?'

'Half an hour to Big Town. Half an hour back.' Vijay patted the old truck as he headed for his vehicle. 'Won't take long to get the old girl back on the road.'

'Then we can all be home by evening.' Claudia raised her hand in farewell as Vijay left.

'This jacket,' said Dennis. He raised it to his nose and sniffed.

'What are you doing?' said Clive.

Dennis let the jacket droop. 'It's very clean.'

'Ivan wasn't actually fire fighting in it,' said Claudia. 'He waved and threw sweets at the children. Hardly going to get it dirty doing that.'

'I suppose so.'

'Let me look.' Clive gestured for the jacket, and Dennis handed it over. 'It isn't that clean. See?' He turned the jacket so that the others could see the lining where a smudge of dirt marked the back. 'I reckon we might have pulled it off him as he was lying on the ground.'

'It's funny, but I don't remember us doing that. It's all a blur.' Claudia tugged the jacket from Clive and turned it around. 'It's dirtier than you reckon, Dennis. You need your glasses on.'

'Okay, okay. It's dirty.'

Claudia frowned. 'I wore it last year, but I didn't wash it because I couldn't find it. That could be my dirt. Sorry.'

Dennis shook his head. 'You didn't collapse while you were wearing it, Claudia.'

'No.' Claudia shrugged and squeezed the padding of the jacket. 'I guess I'm made of tougher stuff than Ivan was.'

'We'd already guessed that.' Dennis grinned. 'You're as hard as nails.'

Claudia took a step toward her teammate, but Rosemary stopped her with an outstretched hand. 'That suit belongs to the brigade?'

'Definitely.' Claudia held the jacket out to show faint black writing on its hem. 'See? B. T. C. F. T. Big Town Country Fire Truck. That's us.'

Rosemary frowned. There were no initials on the Santa jacket hanging on her coat rack.

Dennis ran his fingers through his hair. 'So, we have a jacket, a beard and a hat. Now we can play Santa.'

Clive leaned back against the truck and swept his hand out. 'Who to?'

In the time they had been standing there, the sun had risen higher, and its rays were not completely blocked by the thin clouds overhead. The shade from the expansive Exceptional Tree had shrunk, leaving a small huddle of tourists sucking on a range of cold drinks under its cover.

'Are you expecting more tourists this afternoon?' Dennis asked Rosemary.

'We have no control over that.' Rosemary pointed to a bus parked on Goldmarket Road, who had opened its doors for returning occupants. 'I'm frankly surprised that anyone is out today, but we opened early for that very reason. This is the hottest Christmas Eve in years.'

'Absolutely,' said Clive. 'And it was predicted.'

Claudia grinned at him. 'Your instincts told you that?'

He glared at her. 'Yes. And I checked the advice from the meteorology bureau. I had to make sure.'

'Maybe we should have gone back with Vijay, then.' Dennis wiped his forehead. 'None of us are keen to play Santa, even if there were hordes of people here.' He pointed at The Sweet Potato. 'I think I'll go get something to eat while we're waiting for Vijay. The coffee's worn off and Clive isn't sharing his goodies.'

'They're for Christmas Day.'

'You'll have eaten most of them by tomorrow.' Dennis grinned. 'Wait until I see Kath.'

'When do you ever see Kath?'

'I could go to your house especially.'

'Don't you dare.'

Clive's shout was lost in a sudden swoosh of hot wind. Rosemary turned her gaze to him. He was staring down Dennis who didn't notice, distracted by Claudia as she threw the Santa suit back into the truck. There were crumbs down Clive's shirt and, because he was panting slightly in the heat, she could see something orange stuck in his front tooth. He noticed her looking and passed a hand over his face. When it dropped, the hardness had gone.

'Okay,' said Dennis as Claudia slammed the back passenger door closed. 'I'm getting something to eat. Maybe once I get some tucker into me, I'll feel more of the Christmas spirit.'

'Might as well,' said Clive. He waved his hand at the truck. 'The Santa suit is there, and someone can put it on if a busload of littlies comes along.'

'It's funny,' said Claudia. 'I don't think I put it back there after Ivan was taken away.' She paused, thinking. 'Mind you, everything happened in such a rush once Ivan went down, I can't quite remember.'

'You're right, Claudia.' Dennis wiped his face again. 'All that action, plus the heat. My brain has gone to mush. A bit like yours is every day, Clive.'

'Oh, ha ha.' Clive shook his head. 'But Claudia is

correct. Anyone could have stuffed that suit in the truck for all we know. The last twenty-four hours are fuzzy.'

'And about to get fuzzier if I don't get out of this sun.' Dennis pulled out a hanky and wiped his face with it. 'Come on, you two. Let's go.' He glanced at Rosemary. 'Can I shout you a drink?'

'No,' said Rosemary. 'I'll get back to my shop.'

'Goodo.' Dennis herded his colleagues on with outstretched arms. 'Once I've had a drink, I'm heading to the bookshop to pass the time. We'll take our fuzzy heads away for now.'

Rosemary watched until they entered The Sweet Potato, then headed back to The Preserved Mulbury. 'Fuzzy?' she said to Sunny as the cat greeted her at the jangling door. 'I'd guess that at least one of them is as clear as glacial water.'

EIGHT

Jasper Lu twisted his hair back into its bun as, through his shop window, he watched Rosemary Exeter walk back across the road to The Preserved Mulbury. She had a sunflowery dress on that caught on her legs as she went, and her long braid hung neatly over her shoulder. He sighed, and let his hands drop to his side. She looked so *contained*. He wished she was more in need of company. *My company,* he thought, with an embarrassed laugh to himself.

The Read Mulbury had been empty for an hour as the remaining tourists lunched on Rakisha's vegan sushi, Kelly's sandwiches or Franco's pies. Jasper knew it wouldn't be long before they got sick of the heat and wandered over to the shops under the veranda to seek a cooler space until they boarded their bus or climbed into their air-conditioned cars to head home. The bookstore was wedged effectively between Rosemary's shop and Patricia's and evaded most of the heat. Perhaps it was the extra lining from the rows and piles and boxes of books that took up every spare centimetre.

Jasper sat back again behind his shop counter and

picked up the book he'd been reading until he'd glimpsed Rosemary. He read two paragraphs and put it down. Something was making it difficult to concentrate, and it wasn't entirely the spectacle of Rosemary through the window. It was more that he had a notion that Rosemary was up to something. She'd gone past his shop as he'd been serving customers earlier in the morning with a bag he knew she'd taken to Patti, as he'd heard the door squeal next door. Perhaps the bag was full of old aprons rather than anything suspicious? He really wouldn't know. 'Rosemary Exeter is harder to read than a Patrick White novel,' he said into the silence of the shop.

From his position upside down on the couch in Jasper's living area, Snowy gave a little yip as if in agreement.

The door to The Read Mulbury sighed heavily as someone pushed it open. 'Oh, it's so much better in here. The inside of our truck is hot enough to fry an egg.'

'Quite a scorcher, isn't it?' said Jasper as Dennis came to stand under the ceiling fan.

'You can say that again.' Dennis plucked his shirt away from his chest. 'Thanks for this. I'll get it washed and sent back to you.'

'That's fine. You can keep it if you like. It was an old one I had so I don't need it back.'

Dennis stepped up to the counter and placed a long brown package on it. 'That's generous of you. Maybe next time I'm passing through I'll return it. It'll be Christmas again before we know it, and we won't have Ivan to play Santa.' He tapped the parcel. 'Talking about Santas, this was hanging on your door handle.'

Jasper picked up the flat square package. It was wrapped in the pages of an old comic and tied off with a gold bow. 'What is it?'

'No idea. Looks like you have a friend.' Dennis grinned. 'Maybe it's the lady we stayed with last night. The way you look at her, my bet is that you'd like to be more than friends.'

Jasper ducked his head to put the parcel underneath the counter, hoping that the dimness of the shop interior would hide the heat flooding his face. He fussed around with the parcel to allow a moment of calm, before standing straight again. 'Can I help you with a particular title?'

'Well,' said Dennis, turning to study the labelling on the nearest shelves, 'my greatest reading pleasure is horror, which was about the only thing I had in common with Ivan. Got any Bram Stoker prize finalists?'

Horror wasn't Jasper's favourite genre by any means, but luckily, he'd received a box of old titles from a passer-by recently that he'd found shelf room for. 'Here,' he said, leading Dennis to a discrete corner.

'Great range,' said Dennis. 'This'll help me pass the time.' He pulled a book from the shelf and showed Jasper the cover. 'The very one I need. "Vengeance". This was very definitely *not* Ivan's favourite.'

Jasper pulled back a bit from the dripping red font of the title word. 'Oh?'

'No.' Dennis chuckled. 'I guess he didn't want to believe that anything he did would catch up with him, which is not what happened in this cracker of a revenge story.'

'You like revenge stories?'

'Doesn't everyone?' Dennis leaned back on the shelf and opened the book. 'There is nothing more satisfying than someone getting their just dues.'

Jasper frowned, but Dennis offered no more explanation. 'I'll get a chair for you, so you'll be more comfortable browsing.'

Jasper went to a chair he had by the door and picked it

up. Before he could move it, a gust of wind cranked the door open, causing a flurry of advertising pamphlets to scoot into the surrounding air. He pushed at the door until it closed. 'That wind is getting really strong.'

Dennis came out from behind the shelf to stand at the window. He frowned heavily. 'Strong and nasty. It's turned into a real fire danger day.' He pulled out his phone and tapped the screen. 'Nothing yet. I hope it stays that way.'

They watched on for a little while until the dust settled in Goldmarket Square. 'Well,' Dennis said finally, 'not much I can do about it, not with a broken fire truck.' He took the chair from Jasper. 'I think I'll hang around here until Vijay comes back.'

'Vijay?'

'The mechanic.' Again, Dennis glanced at his phone. 'He should be back soon.'

'You're welcome to stay as long as you like. Well, until closing time. Even beyond then, if you need to.'

'Thanks, mate.' Dennis lugged the chair to the horror books and sat down to read.

Now that Dennis had pointed out the imminent danger, Jasper found he couldn't tear himself away from the window. The wind gusted forcibly, making the branches of The Exceptional Tree fling about in a manner that didn't suit the gigantic ancient gumtree. Dust whipped around the Square, making people cover their eyes. A lone plastic chip packet scuttled down the road and Jasper hoped that Mrs Lionel hadn't seen it, or she'd be chasing it all the way to Big Town.

Across the road, Clive was at the truck, not at the opened bonnet but leaning into the back seat from the ground so that Jasper could only see the legs of Clive's red trousers. The wind kept threatening to close the truck's door, and Clive had wedged a hip against. It seemed that Clive was looking for something. Jasper kept seeing things being flung from the back seat to the front.

'Blast!'

The quick shout came from Dennis, who reappeared into the centre of the bookshop with his phone aloft.

'Everything alright?' said Jasper.

'There *is* a fire.' Dennis waved his phone as he hurried to the door. 'Not here, but not too far away, either. At the rate that wind is picking up, Mulbury could be in danger.'

'Mulbury has been through bushfires in the past. It was nearly burnt out during Scarlet Tuesday.'

'Oh, yes.' Dennis nodded vigorously even as he pulled the heavy door open. 'I remember that season. Lots of people died. Let's hope we aren't seeing a replay.'

Jasper shivered, despite the heat. Dennis left the old door to close behind him, letting more hot air into the shop. This time, Jasper thought he could detect a hint of smoke in it. He followed Dennis out but turned to go to Rosemary's rather than toward the fire truck. Dennis waved his phone at Clive, but the other man was still engrossed in his cleaning activity. It was Claudia who noticed him first. Jasper saw her sprint across the Square to the truck and stand close to Dennis to peer at the phone.

'Everything okay?'

Rosemary stood outside her door, one hand holding the elbow of the other arm in a loose gesture that made Jasper's heart rate calm immediately.

'Dennis said there's a fire nearby.'

'I know. It came up on my emergency app.' She eyed him. 'You still haven't put that on your phone.'

Jasper felt his face go blotchy. He tried to hide it by looking back at the group of fire volunteers. Clive had pulled his head out of the truck, but stood with his backside against the door. 'I'll put it on today.'

'Good idea. You don't want to go through another summer without knowing what's going on.' She let her arm go and patted him. 'Just because there's a fire nearby doesn't mean it'll get to Mulbury.'

'How are you so calm, Rosemary? Nothing ever ruffles you.'

She squinted at him briefly, and Jasper glimpsed a darkness in her hazel eyes that was immediately replaced by her usual shrewdness. 'There's no need to be ruffled, Jasper. That's why I'm not.'

He could hardly argue with her. Instead, he pointed to the fire volunteers. 'They aren't having much luck.'

'Sounds like the truck will be fixed shortly, then they'll be on their way.'

'Were they pleasant guests last night?'

'After you left, they fell asleep.'

'Pleasant enough, then.'

Rosemary said nothing.

'What's going on?'

She arched one eyebrow. 'What do you mean by that?'

He stepped closer to her. 'I know I'm not as observant as you, Rosemary, but I did notice that you are taking a more than casual interest in our fire fighters, which is probably why you're standing outside your shop rather than inside where it's cooler.'

'They are the morning's entertainment.' She tipped her head in the truck's direction. 'See?'

Dennis and Claudia were standing toe to toe, Dennis waving his arms around and Claudia standing with hers crossed tightly in front of her. Clive was circling them like an umpire in a boxing match. He reached in to separate them, but had no luck. After a minute, the argument stopped, and Dennis shrugged while Claudia moved off to answer her phone. Clive's face was flushed, and he lifted his shirt up to wipe his face.

'They bicker a lot,' said Jasper. 'I noticed that last night.'

'If they aren't careful, they'll end up too hot.'

'Like Ivan.'

'They won't get as hot as Ivan.'

'What do you mean?'

She turned to him. 'He was wearing a heated vest. Someone tried to cook him.'

'One of them?' Jasper jerked his thumb at the small crowd in front of the truck.

Rosemary said nothing.

Jasper chewed his lip for a moment, then held up a finger. 'Hang on.' He bolted back to his shop, searched among the cushions of the chair he'd given Dennis, and ran out onto the footpath again. 'See?'

Rosemary held the book with both hands, staring at the glossy front cover. 'No.'

'No? What?'

'I don't see.'

Jasper tapped the book. 'The title. Look what it's called.'

'"Vengeance".'

'Yes, Dennis was reading it.'

'Right.'

Jasper took the book back. 'It was the way he talked about it. He said that revenge is the best type of story. Don't you think it could make him a suspect?'

But Rosemary didn't seem to be listening. She stared at Claudia, who had finished her phone call and was standing stunned, her gaze locked on the men near the truck.

NINE

Ignoring Jasper's question, Rosemary crossed the scorching asphalt and went over to Claudia. The woman hadn't moved and didn't seem to notice Rosemary until she touched her arm. 'What's happened, Claudia?'

'Oh no, is she doing it again?' Clive marched over and stood with his hands on his hips, looking at his colleague. 'Claudia, snap out of it.' He clicked his fingers in Claudia's face until she blinked.

'Don't, Clive.'

'Well, it's the only thing that gets you out.'

'I wasn't *in*.'

'Yeah?' Clive shrugged at Rosemary. 'She can't help it, poor love. Gets a bit affected when there's a touch of smoke in the air.'

'I do not,' said Claudia, tattoos bulging as she crossed her arms.

'You do. But it's okay. We understand. We were there, too.'

'Are you talking about the incident when you were burned?' asked Rosemary.

'Horrible, it was.' Clive shook his head. 'It was a long recovery for all of us. Claudia still gets a few flashbacks.'

'Clive,' said Claudia harshly, 'I don't. I used to, but I'm over it.' She sniffed. 'If I was to be affected by that tiny whiff of smoke in the air, what use would I be in a fire crew?'

Clive nodded, a slow smile on his face. 'Well, that's why you're driving the truck for Santa now, isn't it?'

Claudia's jaws tightened. 'You can talk, Clive. Don't see you taking any frontline jobs, eh?'

Rosemary put her hand up. 'That's not what happened just now. Claudia, you finished that phone call and looked like you'd heard bad news.'

'I did.' Finally, Claudia relaxed her arms. 'Vijay is caught on the road and can't get through because of the grass fire they're fighting. That's the smoke you can smell, Clive, and that's the fire on the alert.'

'Great,' said Dennis, wandering up to his colleagues. 'We're stuck here until he gets through.'

Claudia shook her head. 'We should have tried harder to fix it ourselves.'

'We *couldn't*, right? We needed a mechanic.' Dennis was ready to take the argument further, but Claudia had already turned away.

'I'm ringing the brigade to tell them we'll be late.'

The wind whipped across the Square again, and this time Rosemary caught the acrid odour of burning grass. She couldn't see any smoke plumes, but the thin clouds colouring the sky made it difficult to detect anything. A car she'd already seen this morning made its way onto Gold-market Road, possibly turned around on its way back to Big Town by the emergency services. Its occupants didn't look too upset as they got out. In fact, they pointed to The Read Mulbury as if they'd just noticed it and headed inside.

Jasper had to hurry to join them. *If no one can get home for a while,* thought Rosemary, *our Christmas Eve service will extend.*

'Now what's up?' said Dennis as Claudia finished on the phone again. 'Your face is as long as a horse's.'

Rosemary bristled for Claudia, but the fire volunteer shrugged the remark off. 'I told them about the delays with our truck and they told me some news about Ivan. News we would have heard had we been listening to the radio.'

'What news?' said Clive, his hands plunged into his trouser pockets.

'Ivan's death is being treated as suspicious.'

Rosemary watched for any reaction. Claudia stayed looking grim while Dennis's eyes shot wide before settling. Clive shook his head slightly. 'That's absurd,' he said. 'The man got too hot and popped his final cork. What's so suspicious about that on a day that hit a heat record for this time of the year?'

'I don't know,' said Claudia. 'All they said is that his inner body temperature was way hotter than it should have been, even for a Santa in a fat suit. Apparently, unless he'd been jogging or weightlifting in the sun, he shouldn't have got that hot.'

'But he did,' said Dennis. 'I was hot. You were hot. It *was* hot. I think they're barking up the wrong tree.'

'So, you're an expert, are you, Dennis?' Claudia put her hands on her hips. 'You can build houses and fix humans as well?'

'Get on with you, Claudia. You can see it makes no sense.'

'It may not make sense to us, but who are we? I think we have to accept that something was very wrong with Ivan's death.'

In the quiet that followed Claudia's statement, the wind dropped, and the sun shone fiercely through a break in the cloud. Although the wind had been warm, its absence meant that the full strength of the sun beat down on the small crowd. Clive's face glowed red, and he wiped his forearm repeatedly across his brow, staggering a little as he stepped back to lean on the back seat of the truck.

'Okay,' said Dennis. 'That's sad news. Strange news. Nothing we can do about it right now. We need to get this truck moving and get out of here.'

'We can't do either until Vijay gets here. Even if the truck started, the road to Big Town is blocked.'

Dennis thrummed his fingers on his thigh. 'Well, I need something to do.'

'Looks like it's your lucky day.' Claudia pointed to a car that had just pulled up. Three children climbed out and ran to the shade of The Exceptional Tree to wait for their slower parents. 'You get to play Santa.'

Dennis watched the children for a moment. 'Do their parents look rich?'

Claudia glanced back at the car. 'Hard to tell.'

'I'll take the risk.' He pushed Clive aside to get to the Santa suit and hat. 'This weekend was meant to be a major fundraising one. If I can get ten dollars out of their mum and dad, it won't be a complete loss.' He jammed the hat on his head. 'Ready with the electronic transfer gadget?'

Claudia indicated the front of the truck. 'I'll get it. Clive?'

Clive fanned himself with a logbook. 'What?'

'Ready to do your spiel about how we need to raise our own money to buy a new fire truck?'

'What?'

Claudia shook her head, opened the front door of the

truck, and pulled out the collection device. 'You go first, Dennis. I'll bring Clive over in a moment.'

Dennis zipped up the padded Santa jacket and strapped on the ragged beard, transforming himself into the worst Santa Rosemary had ever seen. She stopped him before he made his way to the children, adjusted the beard so that it hid his unshaven cheeks better, pulled the hat down further, and fluffed up the padding in the suit so it was as even as she could get it. 'Better?' said Dennis.

'Ten percent better,' Rosemary said, standing back and eyeing him critically.

'Ah well.' He winked at her as he walked away. 'At least this Santa is alive.'

'Did he really say that?' Claudia shook her head and followed, taking Clive by the arm and dragging him with her.

Rosemary shaded her eyes with a hand to watch them, half expecting the children to run screaming back to the car, but as they walked, the fire volunteers took on their parts. Dennis's gait changed from his usual purposeful stride to a rollicking lope, and he called out a merry 'Ho, ho, ho!' as he went. Claudia carried the electronic device in one hand, so she hid it discretely behind her leg. Clive was the most impressive. He drew himself up as they approached the Tree, smiling and chuckling at Dennis as if the scruffy Santa was the jolliest of all Santas, and parked himself near the children's parents, who were watching the arrival of the fire crew with some trepidation. Rosemary heard the light murmur of Clive's voice as he leaned in to tell them, she supposed, the sorry story of the fire brigade and how they needed a new truck. She left them to it and walked back across the road to Sunny.

The orange cat wasn't the only one waiting for Rosemary, though.

'Hello, dear.' Mrs Lionel sat at the shop counter with her elbows resting on its surface.

'Are you alright?'

'You had some customers. I ducked in here to serve them and now I can't be bothered going back to my shop.' The older woman leaned back and fluffed her hair from her neck. 'Will this heat ever be gone?'

'Tomorrow. That's what they said.'

'We'll have to suffer through today, then.' Mrs Lionel waved a finger towards the front windows. 'What's going on over there, then?'

'They're playing Santa.'

'But we've got the jacket from the Santa suit.'

'We've got another jacket. There was already one in the truck.'

'Ah. We were correct. This one is not their usual Santa costume.'

'No.' Rosemary lifted her heavy braid from her shoulder and let it fall down her back.

'Anything else?'

'They've been told that Ivan's death is suspicious.'

'Well, we know what that means.'

Rosemary studied Mrs Lionel's placid face. 'We do?'

'Someone will look for the jacket that caused it all.' Mrs Lionel peered into Rosemary's living area. 'Where is it, dear?'

'I hung it back up behind my raincoat.'

'Alright then.' The older woman eased herself off the stool. 'Keep it hidden, as I know you will. It could be time to call Geoffrey.'

'I thought that. Do you know whether he's on holidays?'

'Like the dedicated police officer he is, I doubt whether he's had a holiday at Christmas time in all the decades he's been working.'

'Is that a yes or a no?'

'Geoffrey is an old friend, Rosemary Exeter, but I don't keep close tabs on his everyday movements.' Mrs Lionel tapped her finger on the counter. 'Not like I do yours, anyhow. Why don't you ring him and see?' She rubbed her temple. 'I'll go back to my shop now, but I don't think I'll stay open for much longer.'

Rosemary noted the puffiness under Mrs Lionel's eyes. 'That's a good idea. Finish up and come back here. You can keep me company from my couch.'

'That will be lovely.' Mrs Lionel patted Rosemary's arm as she went by. 'I must say, if you can't have your family around you at Christmas time, it's wonderful having your friends. Now, ring Geoffrey.'

Rosemary held the door for Mrs Lionel as she left, then let it jangle slowly closed. Santa was still entertaining the children in the Square. She could see the father taking snapshots on his phone while the mother, with Claudia standing close, was fishing around in her handbag. *Looking for her credit card,* Rosemary thought. She dialled Detective Inspector Geoffrey's number and left a message asking him to ring back.

Ten minutes later, the family burst into The Preserved Mulbury, startling Sunny, who had ventured into the shop and was doing a delicate sniffing exercise along the windowsill. The cat sat back with her ears flattened as the door jangled furiously.

'Hey,' called the father to Rosemary, who was stacking a shelf on the back wall. 'Do you know those fire fighters? I saw you standing with them.'

Rosemary put the last jar of lavender vinegar on the shelf and spun around. 'I know who they are.'

'Well.' The father put his hands over his youngest child's ears. 'Santa's having a bit of *difficulty* with the other person.' He jerked his head repeatedly toward the window. 'Perhaps his elves are being slow?'

'Dad.' The child pulled free. 'I know that's not really Santa.'

'Right. Well. Anyway. This lady is going to help Santa, so he's ready for his sleigh tonight.'

'Dad, only the real Santa rides a sleigh tonight.'

The man widened his eyes at Rosemary, who looked out the window to where Claudia had Dennis up against the bonnet of the truck and appeared to be trying to rip the jacket off him.

'I'll go and see them.' Rosemary paused. 'Anything you want to buy before I go?'

'We're heading off to the city now,' said the man, ushering his family out the door. 'Thanks anyway.'

Rosemary followed them out and ran across the road to where Claudia now had Dennis in a headlock while Clive gripped the Santa beard, stretching it to the full length of the elastic. 'What are you doing?'

'She's gone mad,' said Clive, panting. 'Claudia, let the man go!'

'Let him go?' Claudia squeezed Dennis a bit more. 'After what he said?'

'It's true!' wheezed Dennis. 'You called him fat and useless.'

'I didn't.' Claudia gave another squeeze, then let Dennis go. 'It wasn't me.'

'But I heard you.' Dennis snatched the beard from Clive. 'That's what you said.'

'It was *Ivan*, you moron. Tell him, Clive.'

Clive's mouth curled. 'It wasn't Claudia, Dennis. It was Ivan.'

'Ivan?' Dennis rubbed his throat. 'But it sounded like Claudia.'

Claudia huffed. 'Well, thanks a lot for thinking I sounded like a skinny little weasel of a man.'

Dennis's face, already an unhealthy red, went darker. 'Sorry, Claudia. And I'm sorry, too, Clive.'

Clive lifted his hand. 'It was years ago.'

'Well, I knew Ivan was a nasty person, so I should have known it was him.' Dennis glanced apologetically at Claudia. 'But, you know, Claud. You do have a temper.'

Rosemary coughed. 'Everything alright now?'

'Oh, so sorry, Rosemary.' Clive gave a mirthless smile. 'All good now.'

Claudia shook herself off. 'It's not, you know. Even with Ivan dead, we're not a team.' She stared at Dennis, then Clive. 'I thought it would be different.' She shrugged and walked off across the road.

'Let her go,' said Clive as Dennis went to go after her. 'Like I said, she's not herself. So sorry, Rosemary, that you had to witness that. You go back to the shop. We'll see Claudia in a tic. Come on, Dennis. Sit in the truck for a minute.'

Rosemary left them to it, but not before she caught Clive's narrow-eyed look at the distraught woman making her way to Patricia's.

TEN

Patti Yale sat at her sewing table, putting the last stitches into her Christmas Day costume. The gold blouse had been a very lucky find, one that she would be eternally grateful to Kelly for locating in the scrap bin of an op shop at the edge of Big Town. One sleeve had gone completely, and Patti would have removed the other except for remembering Cate Blanchett's one-shouldered gown at the Oscars in 2005. There was no one more elegant than Cate Blanchett, except perhaps Rosemary Exeter (if she'd dress less like a farmer and more like an actor), and Patti shivered in anticipation at wearing the revamped shirt tomorrow.

The door squealed as a customer thumped in, and Patti finished her work, spreading the garment out on her table as she stood. It was a fine job, and she stared at it lovingly for a moment too long. The customer had made their way right up to the counter before she noticed them. 'Oh,' she said. 'Hello. I'm so sorry to hear what happened.'

The woman shifted uncomfortably from foot to foot. Patti immediately understood why. 'Those big, black boots must be awful on a hot day like today,' she said. 'Are they part of your uniform?'

The woman glanced down, as if she'd just noticed she had feet. 'You get used to them. I wear merino wool socks which soak up any sweat.'

Patti nodded. 'Merino wool makes the best fabric. I made a swimsuit out of a picnic rug once. It was sensational.'

The woman's eyebrows twisted, but then she smiled and thrust out her hand. 'Claudia,' she said.

'Patti,' said Patti.

'Patti of Patricia's?'

'That's me,' said Patti happily. 'Although we could have called the shop Patti and Gerry's, but it sounded too much like a comedy duo.'

'Gerry?'

'He's my husband.' Patti waved toward the living area of the house where Gerry was doing the dishes at the sink. 'He makes an excellent cup of tea. Would you like one?'

'No, but thanks for asking.' She put two soft parcels on the counter, each decorated with expansive glittery red bows. 'These were hanging on the door handle outside.'

'Oh.' Patti touched the presents with a thimble-capped finger. 'They must be our secret Santa presents. How wonderful!'

'Lucky you.'

'Oh, yes, we are lucky in this town. Now, was there anything in particular you were after?' Patti swivelled to the left and touched a mannequin. 'I mainly do bespoke creations for customers but sometimes I, you know, *create*.' She fingered the sleeve of the pantsuit on display.

'I don't think I've ever created anything in my life.'

'Oh, but you have.'

'Sorry?'

Patti reached out and touched the skin of Claudia's arm with one fingertip. 'You had a canvas, and you filled it in.'

Claudia's sleeve of tattoos was bright in the shop's lighting. She lifted her arm and twisted it this way and that. Patti saw a rolling account of a panting dog, a rose, a smiling woman and a twist of vine. 'I didn't actually design anything here,' said Claudia. 'Someone else inked me.'

'Well, yes, just as I didn't weave any of the fabrics in my shop. But you chose the designs and they're meaningful to you. They aren't a collection of other people's fancies.'

'No, you're right. They're *my* fancies.' Claudia touched the dog. 'This is my first pup, Clea. She lived for nineteen years. And this one.' She slid her finger to the woman and paused. 'Well, this is my mum. She was one special woman.'

'See?' said Patti, rocking to her toes and back. 'You chose beautifully. They fit so well together.'

Claudia stared a moment longer at her arm before letting it drop. 'You know, you are very kind. Thank you. I needed to hear that today.'

'You are very welcome.' Patti cupped the curls at her neck. 'I'll let you have a look around and see if anything captures your eye.'

She left Claudia to browse and went back to the gold shirt. There was the tiniest hole in its front, one that could be covered by a funky addition, or made invisible by good mending. She chose the funky option, pulling out a box of allsorts from under the counter, and started rummaging through the buttons, ribbons, and doilies within. Sadly, there was no silk thread, but there was a tiny red diamante bird that must have been a brooch once upon a time. *Divine,* thought Patti, and sat down to sew it on. She forgot about the shop altogether as she fastened the bird, thinking instead of jewelled wings and shiny eyes. Claudia's knock on the counter made her jump.

'Sorry,' Claudia said, 'but do you have any, you know, blazers? Jackets, maybe? Something to throw over a T-shirt when you're going out to make yourself respectable?'

'Oh, I love a satin-lined blazer.' Patti gave the little bird a last tap and stood up. 'I have a rack of unknowns here.'

'Unknowns?'

'Yes. Garments I haven't yet decided what to do with yet.' Patti tugged at a portable rack hiding at the back of the shop until it came out into the interior. 'Sometimes I know exactly what to do with a new piece, but other times I have to wait until the customer comes along to make the garment suit them.' She eyed Claudia thoughtfully. 'Did you have an occasion in mind?'

'Christmas Day, actually.' Claudia shrugged. 'Followed not long after by a funeral. Is it possible to wear the same thing on two very different occasions?'

'Yes, yes, easily done. What we need are some additions that can be removed or changed according to what you're doing. Did you have a base colour in mind?'

'I don't have anything in mind, except that I've always wanted a blazer.'

'An extremely versatile garment in any wardrobe. Let's see.' Patti stepped close to study Claudia's face. The fire volunteer's skin was tanned and full of fine lines gathered after years of outdoor activity. Her eyes were summer sky blue and stood out against the ruddiness of her face like pools of water in a desert. 'You know, I might have the perfect piece.'

It took a moment to find the blazer among the packed rack of unknowns. Each garment had been cleaned and hung, then grouped into type. Even so, several jackets, coats and blazers hid the one Patti was looking for. 'Ah. Here. Perfect.'

'Oh, yes,' said Claudia as Patti handed her the king-fisher blue blazer. 'Where on earth did you find that?'

'I suspect it was in the church's lost property box in Big Town.' Patti smoothed the lapel. 'I discover such wonderful things when they have their end-of-year sale. You can see from the careful way they stitched the lining that it is a good quality item. Unfortunately, though, it's a little drab.'

'It is?'

'Well, it's not *you* yet, is it?' Patti twisted Claudia's hand so that the garment swung around. 'If you wear that now, you'll turn into a replica of a staid old lady.'

Claudia ran a hand through her silver-tipped hair. 'I will?'

'Oh yes. We must do something about that. What do you think about attaching a swirl?'

'A swirl?'

'Yes.' Patti twirled her finger. 'I've got some fine braid here that we can shape into a pattern to sew on the sleeve.' She landed her finger on Claudia's arm again. 'Is that vine significant?'

'The vine?' Claudia rolled her arm so that the tattoo came into view. 'Well, yes. It's my grandmother's climbing rose, the one she had at the back of her house when I was a kid. Most people think it's only a random vine. How did you know?'

'Because the others you've had inked are special to you. I don't think you're a random type.' Patti turned to her allsorts box and pulled out a long length of deep sapphire braid. 'What do you think of this?'

'It's... I don't know what to think.'

'I'll show you what I had in mind.' Patti took the jacket

back and placed it carefully on her sewing table with the back facing up. She studied Claudia's arm again, then twisted the braid before pinning it onto the blazer. The shop was quiet as she worked apart from the swish of the fans, and when she finally stood back, it was like a trance had broken. 'There.'

The braid hurtled from the left shoulder of the jacket, bending and flexing as it went, until it reached the diagonal hip. Claudia leaned her arm against it, and the vines were in parallel. She shook her head and blinked rapidly.

'It's okay, sweetie,' said Patti, gazing at her creation. 'It often happens when I work with clients. People get all choked up with their emotions. Now, before I go any further, slip it on and I'll see if there are any other adjust-ments to be made before I finish the braid.'

Claudia straightened and let herself be dressed by Patti, who nipped in the material here and there, and frowned at a wonky button. The fire volunteer still had said nothing by the time Patti was ready to sew. When Patti looked at her, Claudia's bottom lip was trembling. 'Gerry,' called Patti. 'Could you make some tea?'

'Yes, my love. Coming right up.'

While Gerry prepared the tea, Patti took the blazer and steered the silent Claudia into a chair and sat back at her table. Now and then, she glanced at the woman, who was recovering. At least her lip was still again, and the moisture had dried from her eyes.

'Here it is.' Gerry came out of the kitchen, walking slowly with a tray held stiffly in front of him. He caught sight of Claudia, nodded briefly, and continued until he could set the tray on the shop counter. 'The teapot is bare, sorry, as I shrunk the tea cosy in the wash and I'm afraid we've run out of ginger snaps.'

'Franco's tarts are in the fridge.' Patti leaned towards Claudia. 'Gerry was so upset about the cosy. Not even Mrs Lionel could salvage it. Would you like a lemon tart?'

Claudia had to clear her throat before her words became audible. 'Lemon. Yes. My favourite.'

Gerry ducked out again to fetch tarts, but Claudia's drought had broken. She stood and poured the tea, leaving a cup for Patti well out of knocking range, and taking her own back to her seat. When Gerry appeared, he sat in the chair beside her. 'Help yourself,' he said, putting a plate of tiny lemon tarts on an upturned basket in front of them. 'Franco is the best pastry chef for two hundred kilometres.'

'Oh, more than that, Gerry sweetie.' Patti plucked a pin from the braid and stabbed it into a cushion. 'He would beat most of them in the city.'

'Mulbury is an interesting little place,' said Claudia, reaching for a tart. 'Out of the way but full of geniuses.'

'Country places often are,' said Gerry. 'It's only that city folk can't see beyond their smog.'

'You've never been here before?' asked Patti.

'No.' Claudia took a bite of tart and closed her eyes for a moment. 'Delicious! Mulbury isn't on our list of Santa visits. We were passing through when...' She crammed the rest of the sweet into her mouth.

'Sad business,' said Gerry. 'Horrible to have a teammate die right in front of you.'

'How are you holding up?' said Patti, shifting the blazer to work on a section of lining that had come adrift. 'What a shock for you all.'

'We aren't too bad.' Claudia licked her finger. 'It was a shock, but it wasn't like Ivan was well liked. And it was quick. A good way to go.'

'Sounded a bit horrible,' said Gerry. 'Death by being

cooked.' He sighed and fanned himself with a pair of resur-
rected shorts that had been resting on his chair. 'Mind you,
could be anyone of us today.'

Patti re-threaded her needle. 'Except that he had that
vest on.'

'Vest?' Claudia swallowed. 'What do you mean?'

Patti held up her needle and thread, the fine blue
dangle of it catching the light. 'The Santa suit had been
padded out.'

'They always are.'

'Not in this way. Although, if Santa had really travelled
from the North Pole to come to Australia, he might have
wanted to be warmer. Initially, anyway.'

'Patti,' said Gerry, 'you're not making any sense.'

'The Santa jacket, Gerry.' Patti put her needle down.
'Someone had sewn in one of those battery-heated vests.
You know the ones. They advertise them for when people
go hiking in the mountains.'

'Someone had...?' Gerry shook his head.

Patti smiled at him. *He's so endearing,* she thought.
'Gerry, Rosemary believes that someone did this deliberately. Santa got stuck in his suit and his blood boiled until
he was dead.'

In the quiet that followed, Patti finished attaching the
braid and held the blazer up for Claudia to see, but the fire
volunteer stared over Patti's shoulder, her mouth slightly
open.

'Claudia?'

Claudia put a hand to her pale cheek, blinked, and
focused again on Patti. 'You say Rosemary thinks it was
deliberate?'

'Oh yes, and we pretty much go on everything Rosemary says, don't we, Gerry?'

Gerry nodded. 'Rosemary Exeter is a most astute woman.'

Patti shook the blazer slightly, and it finally caught Claudia's attention. She reached out with both hands, and Patti laid it over her arms. Claudia stood and slipped it on, doing up the single row of three buttons, and pulling scraps of hair out of the collar. 'Oh,' said Patti, 'it belongs to you now. You can pin a poinsettia on it for Christmas and a chrysanthemum for the funeral.'

Claudia ran her hand down the blazer's sleeve. 'Strange. It makes me feel good.'

'Clothes can do that, but only if you have the ones for you.' Patti stood, swivelled on her ballet flats, making her skirt fly around her. 'It took me a while to find what I felt comfortable in.'

Claudia wiped an eye. 'I have never found anything for me until now. Thank you.'

Patti waved a hand around. 'Don't thank me. I get more out of the creation that you get out of the wearing.'

Claudia undid the blazer and let it fall from her shoulders before hanging it carefully on the back of the chair.

'Another tart, perhaps?' Gerry held the plate up, and Claudia sat back down to take a sweet.

'Sorry,' she said, 'I got distracted. You were describing Rosemary. How on earth would she know that the Santa jacket Ivan was wearing had a heated vest sewn into it?'

'She got it from the crime scene,' said Patti.

'And then what did she do with it?'

'She brought it here to get my opinion on how it was attached.'

'Rosemary Exeter wanted your opinion?' Gerry grinned. 'There's one for the books.'

'Gerry,' said Patti sternly. 'Why wouldn't Rosemary want my opinion? I am an expert seamstress.'

'That you are, my love.' Gerry's face grew solemn. 'My apologies.'

'Anyway,' said Claudia, 'she brought a jacket to you. So where is it now?'

'I assume that Rosemary still has it with her. Unless, of course, she's given it to Geoffrey.'

'Geoffrey? The bookshop owner?'

Patti gave a tinkling laugh. 'Oh no. The bookshop owner is Jasper. *Geoffrey* is a detective. You could hardly get them more mixed. Geoffrey is tall and broad and slightly gruff-looking with short-cropped hair, whereas Jasper Lu cuts a fine, slim figure in a pair of jeans and a T-shirt, and his hair is dark.'

'Not sure about the man-bun he's toting these days,' said Gerry.

'It's hot, Gerry. If you had hair that long, you'd be putting it up as well.'

Gerry touched his balding pate. 'I haven't seen Geoffrey around for a while.'

'Rosemary might still have the jacket then,' said Claudia, staring into the depths of her tea.

'Most likely. I mean, it is Christmas Eve, isn't it?' Gerry stretched his legs. 'Geoffrey's probably got other things to tidy up today, and he knows the jacket will be safe at Rosemary's.'

Claudia put her cup down heavily. 'I'd better see whether the truck is going again.' She stood, banging her knee on a basket as she did and making Gerry grab at the cup sitting there. 'Thank you.'

Patti knelt to help Gerry, hearing the squeal of the door

as Claudia went outside. She picked up the plate of tarts and sat back on her heels. 'That's odd,' she said.

'It's odd, alright.' Gerry plucked the last tart from the plate. 'I rarely get the last of Franco's tarts.'

'Yes, you do,' said Patti, resting the plate on her lap. 'But that's not what I meant.'

'What did you mean, dear heart?'

Patti shook a finger at the chair Claudia had been sitting on. 'After all that, she's left the blazer here.'

ELEVEN

After nearly an hour, Dennis was still sitting in the truck. Rosemary helped some sweaty customers choose between apricot and strawberry conserve, keeping half an eye on the figure outside. Clive had disappeared quickly, no doubt promising to return with a cool drink or something to relieve his colleague's stress. To Rosemary's half eye, he had not returned.

She ushered the happy tourists out the door and took off over the road. As she approached the truck, she saw Dennis's head resting at an uncomfortable angle on the back of the seat with his hands loose in his lap. The door was open. Rosemary rapped sharply on it before putting a hand on the man's shoulder.

'Wha...?' he said, head lolling toward her.

'Come on.' She tugged at his shirt. 'It's too hot out here.'

Despite the ugly cloud and the fact that the door was open, the temperature inside the truck was horrifying. Dennis's face had an unhealthy sheen of sweat and, although he moved as she pulled at him, his legs were unco-ordinated. He stumbled out of the truck and nearly went down, saved only by the sudden appearance of Jasper Lu, who caught Dennis before he hit the dust.

'What's wrong with him?' Jasper asked as he flung the man's arm over his shoulder.

'Heat exhaustion.' Rosemary positioned herself under Dennis's other arm. 'Take him to my shop.'

'Where are his friends?'

'Don' av any fends,' slurred Dennis.

Jasper widened his eyes at Rosemary, who shook her head slightly. 'Clive was with him. I have no idea where he is now.'

They dragged Dennis across the road to the bewilderment of the remaining town visitors, who watched the spectacle as if it was a Christmas pageant. Rosemary kicked the door open, making the bell attached to its top jangle frantically and Sunny scoot away from her watchful position in the doorway to the living quarters. They sat Dennis on the couch. Rosemary fetched a flannel and a dish of water to sponge his face while Jasper removed the man's heavy boots.

For a while, they worked in silence. Eventually, Dennis opened his eyes briefly and gave a wan smile. 'Hot,' he said.

'Yes.' Rosemary continued her administrations.

'You're hot,' said Dennis, and closed his eyes again.

Jasper chuckled as he rolled the legs of Dennis's trousers up. 'Watch out for this one when he recovers, Rosemary.'

She frowned at Jasper, feeling an uncomfortable heat in her own cheeks that she put down more to the closeness of the bookshop owner than the fire volunteer's words. She inched away from them both and stood up. 'I'll get him some water.'

By the time she got back with a glass of tepid water,

Dennis had rallied. He sat up straight and looked about him, finally spying Sunny on the windowsill. 'Here, pussy-cat,' he called in a raspy voice, but Sunny glared at him with an expression that read *I'm not going anywhere near you, sweaty stranger*.

'Drink this,' said Rosemary. 'Slowly.'

Dennis sipped at his water. 'Thank you,' he said, resting it on his thigh. 'I don't know what came over me.'

'Do you make it a habit to sit in the sun?'

'No. I sat there because I was tired. Also, because I keep expecting Vijay to come along and get us out of here.' He raised one hand weakly. 'Not because it's a horrible place but, you know, we've spent more time here than we expected.' He let his hand drop. 'Clive said he'd get a drink for us. I don't know. Maybe I fell asleep?'

'I think you'd better wait in here until the mechanic arrives,' said Jasper, lifting the glass to Clive's mouth so that he could take another sip. 'We don't want you to go the same way as your friend.'

'Colleague,' said Dennis.

'Whoever. I suspect you're still in shock over what happened yesterday even if you didn't really like the man.'

'Understatement of the year.' Dennis sipped again. 'But you're right. It wasn't a nice thing to witness.'

'Should we be worried about Clive?'

Dennis shook his head. 'I never worry about Clive. He'll be shmoozing up to that little café owner or her unlucky customers. Clive is pretty single-minded about his own needs.'

'Ivan spread rumours about Clive,' Rosemary said, crouching on the floor. 'That's what you said.'

'Yeah, I did. And *he* did. Ivan had a bad streak which only got worse after the branch came down on us.' Clive sipped his water. 'We got compensated well, although money doesn't compensate for the scars, those on our skin and those in our heads. You saw Claudia, eh? Even so, Ivan was furious that he didn't get any money. He said he witnessed the incident, which wasn't strictly true. He didn't even notice it had happened and drove the truck away. It was the crew behind us that pulled us out.'

'So, he started rumours?'

'He did all sorts of things, but, yeah, the rumours about Clive were the worst.' Dennis drained the glass. 'They were the worst because they weren't actually rumours. It was true what Ivan said, but he still shouldn't have said them.'

'What did he say?' said Jasper, then shook his head. 'Sorry. It's really none of our business. You don't have to tell us.'

'Tell us,' Rosemary said with a sharp glance at Jasper. 'It's important.'

Dennis shrugged. 'It's common knowledge around the brigade, although some believe it and some don't. Clive's been sneaking off to the city to see a *special friend*. Ivan saw him with a woman who looked *very friendly*, if you know what I mean. Kath doesn't know. Despite what Clive says, we think he's scared of Kath and if she found out about his little *rendezvous,* he'd be out on his ear with nothing to show for his decades of abattoir work.'

'What makes you think Clive's scared of Kath?'

'Maybe *scared* is too strong a word, but he does what she says. I'd never believe it possible, but Kath put Clive on a rabbit food diet, and he's lost heaps of weight.'

Rosemary frowned. 'How long ago?'

Dennis thought. 'Well, this time last year he could have passed for a very jolly Santa indeed.'

The soft jangle of the door made Rosemary turn. She

was attuned to the bell's vast range of noises, and this one meant a person had crept quietly in, perhaps because they were feeble but more likely because they were trying to be sneaky. Several jars of pickles had vanished mysteriously in the past via a sly tourist. She walked quietly to the shop, then stepped through the doorway from the house with a deliberate thud onto the floorboards. 'Can I help you?'

'Jeepers!' Claudia stood near a shelf, a hand across her chest. 'You nearly scared the living daylights out of me.'

'You came in very quietly.'

'Did I?' Claudia looked around distractedly, running her hand through her hair and making it stand up haphazardly. 'Is Clive here?'

'No. Dennis is.'

'Okay. Do you know where Clive is? I can't see him at the truck.'

'No. He left Dennis sitting in the sun.'

'Sounds about right.' Claudia tilted her head. 'Is Dennis okay then? You seem very serious.'

'He's better now.'

'Where is he?'

Rosemary showed Claudia through to where Dennis stretched out on the couch, sipping another glass of water. 'Claud,' he said. 'Feeling better?'

'I was fine. It's you who's not. What were you doing sitting in the sun on a day like today?'

'Don't you start.' Dennis scowled at Rosemary. 'I already feel like an idiot. I was waiting for Vijay.' He held up his phone. 'He won't be long.'

Claudia nodded.

As Dennis held his glass out to Jasper for yet another drink, Rosemary watched his companion. Claudia rocked from side to side and was staring around the room as if she'd never seen it before, although she'd spent the entire evening there only yesterday.

'Anything I can help you with?' said Rosemary.

'What?'

'You seem to be looking for something.'

'No, no. I just hadn't noticed how homely this place was.' Claudia shrugged. 'I mean, it's at the back of a shop. It could be very unattractive. When I was a kid, I used to go to the local milk bar and the family there lived in the store rooms out the back. That's what I think of when I see something living where they work.'

'This place has had some work, though, eh?' Dennis took his glass from Jasper again. 'These aren't original plaster walls.'

'No.' Rosemary pointed at the ceiling. 'And this isn't original either. The place had been derelict for many years before I got to it.'

'Well, someone's done a great job.' Dennis's phone dinged as a message came through. 'Ah, here's Vijay now. I'd better go see him.' He put his glass down and tried to rise.

Jasper extended his hand and helped the man up. 'How about I come with you? In case you feel a bit wobbly.'

Dennis staggered a bit on his bare feet, then bent to pick up his shoes. 'Thanks, chum. Seems like I need it. I'll put these on outside.'

Jasper followed the slow-moving Dennis out the door, leaving Claudia and Rosemary standing in the lounge area. Rosemary waited, but Claudia didn't move. 'Tea?' Rosemary said.

'What? Oh, no, thanks. Just had one.'

Rosemary moved to the kitchen area and filled the kettle anyway.

Claudia wandered over to the glass doors at the back of the lounge. She put a hand on one experimentally. 'Still boiling out there.'

Rosemary said nothing but watched from the kitchen.

'When Ivan said the Santa jacket was heavy, I thought it was because he was getting old.' Claudia let her hand fall and turned to Rosemary. 'I mean, we're all old, but he seems the oldest of us all. He was getting thin, lost all his muscles. Apart from sniping at everyone, he didn't have any pastimes. He spent his time away from the brigade sitting around drinking. A waste of space, really.'

'Right.'

'That sounds mean, but for some people it's true. You must have felt that way about someone before.'

Rosemary tried hard not to think of Kelly Flanagan.

'But the jacket really was heavy, wasn't it?' Claudia leaned against the door frame. 'It wasn't the jacket we found in the truck this afternoon. You have the jacket he wore that day.'

Rosemary came out from the kitchen area. 'Yes.'

'Patti said there was a heated vest sewn into it.' Claudia stood straight again. 'Deliberately sewn into it. You think someone did that, and it killed Ivan.'

Rosemary folded her arms across her chest but said nothing.

'And that *someone* has to be one of us.'

'That's not for me to decide.'

'No.' Claudia glanced down at the floor, then up again. 'Can I see it?'

'No.'

'Why not?'

'I'll give it to the police when they get here. Best not to have more fingerprints on it.'

Claudia took a step towards Rosemary. 'It'll have all of our fingerprints on it, anyway. I remember now. We pulled it off Ivan when he collapsed. You took it.'

'Yes.'

Claudia took another step, but the sound of the shop door jangling open stopped her. Rosemary craned her head to see who it was. 'Excuse me,' she said to Claudia. 'You've got a visitor.'

'Claudia?' Dennis called through the shop. 'Come and see Vijay. You need to countersign for his work.'

Claudia hesitated, took a last look around the room, and stomped reluctantly towards Dennis, who had gone outside again. She swivelled at the doorway, making her boots squeak on the polished floor. 'Don't tell anyone else about the Santa jacket,' she said. 'Keep it to yourself. It would be bad to let...' She jerked her thumb towards the truck before hurrying after Dennis.

Rosemary went into The Preserved Mulbury to look out the window. Vijay was bent over the engine, while Dennis waved paperwork at the approaching Claudia. Clive was back, clutching a box from Mullings of Mulbury and standing apart from the others. He was looking, not at the mechanic or his colleagues, but at the row of shops under the veranda.

So who is it, Rosemary thought, *that Claudia didn't want told that the modified Santa suit is with me?*

TWELVE

It was about half an hour before a roar emanated from the truck parked in the Square. It startled a sauntering tourist, whose hat fell off when she jumped. Clive scooped it up and handed it back before turning to talk to Vijay.

Rosemary watched through the window. The day had turned very muggy, and her ceiling fans were again on top speed, making the glass in the old panes rattle rhythmically. She tucked a few strands of escaped hair back into her thick braid and put her hands on her hips. Clive was now talking to Dennis and Claudia, pointing at the truck now and then. Dennis was nodding, but Claudia shook her head and went to walk away. Clive grabbed her arm with a swiftness Rosemary hadn't thought possible for someone of such a normally casual manner. It must have hurt, for Claudia yanked her arm back and rubbed it, stepping in to come almost nose to nose with the man.

The rap on the glass made Rosemary blink. 'Everything all right, dear?' mouthed Mrs Lionel from outside.

Rosemary opened the door for her friend. 'Come in out of the heat,' she said.

Mrs Lionel stepped obligingly in. 'It's hot everywhere I go,' she said, fanning herself with a piece of cloth she pulled from the tote bag on her shoulder. 'It almost makes me wish I had refrigerated air conditioning.'

'No, it doesn't.' Rosemary took the older woman by the shoulders and steered her under the fan. 'You've always said cold air gives you chilblains. Better to move the air around and let it brush against the skin.'

'You are so right.' Mrs Lionel tilted her face toward the ceiling. 'That is much better.' She fanned herself again for a moment, then stopped and held the material out to Rosemary. 'I brought serviettes for tomorrow. See? They're Christmassy ones.'

Rosemary eyed the holly-edged square. 'I was going to use my white linen ones.'

'Well, now you're not.' Mrs Lionel opened the tote bag. 'I found these when I was cleaning up the other day. I have far too many things and I'm trying to disperse them. Eight serviettes and a tablecloth to match.' She fossicked around in the bag. 'Oh, I've forgotten the tablecloth.' She handed the bag to Rosemary. 'I'll get it.'

'It can wait.'

'Best to fetch it now, dear.' Mrs Lionel tapped Rosemary's arm with a knobbly finger. 'There's a chance you'll set the table with an ordinary cloth tomorrow and that won't do for Christmas lunch.'

'It would, you know.'

Mrs Lionel smiled. 'I know. But good to make an effort at Christmas time.' She pulled the door open, letting a cloud of hot air in, and closed it quickly behind her.

Rosemary sat the bag on her shop counter and went back to watching the fire crew. Now Claudia was pointing back at The Preserved Mulbury, but Clive shook his head.

Finally, Vijay stepped up, angling his arm to thrust his watch in their faces, before picking up his tools and striding back to his car. Dennis lifted both his hands, shook his head, and followed. Claudia stared at Clive for a moment longer, then followed Dennis. Vijay revved his vehicle, waited until his passengers had closed their doors, and powered off towards Big Town only to come to a sudden stop outside Patricia's. Claudia ran in and came out with a bag, and the car hooned around the corner. Clive watched their departure, tossed the truck keys in the air to catch, and turned his gaze toward Rosemary's shop.

Inside, Rosemary stepped back involuntarily. The day had dimmed as clouds had thickened, but she hadn't turned on the lights. There was still enough sunshine streaming through the skylight to read the labels on the jars stacked around the walls, and that was really what had mattered. She frowned at herself for trying to hide in the shadows and deliberately went forward again on the pretence of altering the window display. It did not surprise her when Clive headed her way.

'Ah, Rosemary,' he said, as he jangled in. 'Still working and the day is almost finished.'

'When you run your own business, you work all the time, day almost finished, or day just started.'

Clive puffed out a laugh. 'Well, I wouldn't know. I've always worked for wages, good ones at that. Proper meat inspectors are hard to find, and we have to do a lot of travelling.'

'Enjoy your job?'

'Aspects of it. I like the travel.'

'You enjoy being away from home.'

He strolled over to a shelf of pickled beetroot and picked up a jar. 'You know what they say.'

'They say a lot of things.'

'This time it's absence makes the heart grow fonder.'

Immediately, an image of Alasdair flickered into Rosemary's head. She pushed it back into the dark recesses. 'That is a saying I totally disagree with.'

Clive laughed again, the sort of mirthless agreement that bordered on assent. 'Now there's a story behind *that* I would love to hear one day. But no time now.' He put the jar back. 'I've got to be on my way home. Kath's waiting, see. Needs someone to get the punch bowl out of the high cupboard.'

'Goodbye then.'

Clive thrust his hands into his pockets. 'Before I go, though, I've something to collect.'

'Last minute Christmas presents?' Rosemary waved her hand at the shelves. 'Conserves and condiments?'

'As much as I like a good tomato sauce on my pies, I'm afraid I have to say no to your delicious array of goodies. I hate to think what Kath would say if she saw me come home with jars of jam.'

'She's kept you on a strict diet.'

Clive's eyebrows shot up. 'How did you know? Oh, don't tell me. It must have been Dennis or Claudia. They love to tease, especially when I pull out my lunchbox and it's full of celery sticks.' He shook his head ruefully. 'But I must say, Kath's plan worked.' He pulled a hand out of his pocket and patted his belly. 'This used to be the size of Santa's full sack of Christmas happiness. I'm trim now, and plan to keep it that way.'

'For your health.'

He grinned, coming to stand near Rosemary at the shop counter. 'Health *and* happiness. Happiness first, health second.'

'I'm pleased for you.' Rosemary paused. 'You said you had something to collect. Did you leave something here from your sleepover?'

'No, no.' Clive rested his clasped hands on Aunt Lilibeth's recipe book, which Rosemary had left on the counter. 'It wasn't something I left here. It was something you brought here.'

Rosemary skidded the precious book away and placed it on a bookshelf behind her. 'Right.'

'Something you brought back to the house after Ivan's... demise.'

Rosemary said nothing, but kept her eyes fixed on Clive's.

He sighed. 'The Santa jacket, Rosemary.'

'You have a perfectly good Santa jacket in the truck.'

'Yes, we do, but that's not the one that Ivan was wearing.'

'What makes you so sure?'

Clive slid his hands closer to Rosemary, making his whole body lean toward her. 'Well, I can't be one hundred percent sure, but I'm very good at putting two and two together. Also, Claudia gave it away.' He pulled himself back. 'Oh, she's not been right since the accident. Gets a bit shaky now and then, but Claudia never lies. She's salt of the earth, that one. Never lies, but also can't hide the truth.' He walked to the doorway to Rosemary's living quarters. 'She mentioned you getting something examined by the gorgeous seamstress on the corner. Now, Rosemary Exeter, what would that be?'

'Patti does my mending sometimes.'

Clive glanced at her. 'Hardly.' He marched through the doorway and started searching the couch, tossing cushions on to the floor. 'My patience is thin. Where is it?'

Rosemary stood a little way from him, keeping her eyes away from the coat rack with its wet weather gear. Sunny sat up from her position on the windowsill, her waving tail and flattened ears a warning. Rosemary shook her head at the cat. 'It's not there.'

'Clearly.' Clive moved to the drawers in the sideboard. 'I need it, Rosemary. I don't trust you for a moment. You've probably already rung the police.'

'Yes.'

Clive looked over his shoulder at her, his face panicked. 'You stupid woman. Where is it?'

Rosemary folded her arms again. 'Not there, either.'

He pulled the drawer out so it crashed to the floor, sending letters skidding across the floorboards, and spun around. 'If I get caught, I'll deny anything you say.' He waggled his finger at her. 'I've been a volunteer in that fire brigade for thirty-five years. I'm a *pillar* of society! You can't sully me.'

'You sullied yourself by sewing that vest into Ivan's suit.'

'Ha!' Clive grinned again, although his face was pale. 'You cannot prove it was mine. It could be Dennis's or Claudia's.'

'No,' said Rosemary. 'It's yours. The marks on it show that.'

'What?' Clive strode to Rosemary. Behind him, Sunny hissed.

'A person wore the vest who was much larger than Dennis or Claudia. Much larger than you. Now, that is. Not when you had more weight on. Your belly wore the material to a shine.'

Clive's mouth fell open a little, but he shook his head vigorously. 'That's not proof.'

'Perhaps not on its own, but it wouldn't take much

detective work to find out who sewed it on for you. Was it the person who fixes yours tents?'

Clive gave a strangled cry and leapt at Rosemary. She jumped back, slipping on the letters strewn across the floor. Clive grabbed her as she fell backward, twisting as he, too, slipped, and they crashed down, Clive landing on top of her.

For a moment, she couldn't breathe. It wasn't only his fingers searching for her windpipe; it was the bulk of Clive himself. *Kath's diet didn't work that well,* she thought as she punched at his head.

The punches made him slide sideways, but his fingers had her throat. Rosemary hit him as hard as she could, but he only eased off when a ginger ball of fury landed on his back, howling angrily. Clive tried to shuck the cat off, but Sunny had her claws in, and wasn't going anywhere.

Rosemary freed one of Clive's hands. 'Get off,' she said. 'You aren't helping yourself.'

Clive bucked, trying to get rid of Sunny while keeping his weight on Rosemary. 'I'll help myself when you tell me where that jacket is.'

'Why did you do it?' Rosemary wheezed. 'Why did you want Ivan dead?'

'Not dead: out of action.' Clive kicked, but Sunny stayed firm. 'He was going to tell Kath about... well, about a *relationship* I have with a very lovely woman.' He tightened his grip on Rosemary's neck. 'You don't know Kath. She's vengeful. She'd take everything.'

'You were prepared to kill Ivan to save yourself?'

'Not kill! Not kill! Just stop him coming to Christmas lunch and telling Kath.' He heaved again, and this time Sunny went flying. 'Idiot cat!'

From beneath Clive's angry voice, Rosemary heard a

determined, quick jangle of the shop door. She sensed someone crossing the shop and tried to wave her arm, but Clive pinned it down with his elbow. Even so, Rosemary glimpsed Mrs Lionel as she appeared in the doorway. 'Go away,' she said croakily, Clive's forearm on her throat.

'I will,' he said, 'when you give me that Santa suit!'

'I didn't mean you.'

Clive frowned. 'Didn't mean me... what?' He pressed harder, making her choke. 'Don't you see? I can't go until I have that jacket!'

Behind him, Mrs Lionel pointed to her left.

'I don't understand,' Rosemary tried to tell her friend.

'Oh, it's easy.' Clive shifted his weight a little, making Rosemary gasp. 'No jacket, no guilty verdict.'

Clive's face was so close to her own, she could feel his wet breath on her cheeks. She wriggled hard and groped for a weapon, but nothing was within reach.

Mrs Lionel had disappeared from Rosemary's view. Rosemary strained to see where she'd gone, but the room was too dim. It was quiet, too: the only sounds were those of Clive's laboured breathing as he leaned on Rosemary.

'One last chance, Rosemary Exeter. Where is the jacket?'

A shadow moved behind them, but Rosemary's vision was growing darker the heavier the pressure on her throat became. 'One last chance to what, exactly?' she croaked. 'If you kill me, you'll never find it.'

'In a house this size, it's only a matter of time.'

'In a town this small, you'll never get past the front door.' Rosemary twisted to ease his squeeze, relieving it a little.

The shadow moved closer.

'You'll be seen.'

'Won't matter.' Clive grinned. 'What are people going to say if I'm wearing a Santa suit except for *have a Happy Christmas*? No one would tackle a Santa on Christmas Eve.'

'You're so wrong there,' Rosemary said hoarsely, closing her eyes as dizziness dulled her head. 'Mrs Lionel would.'

THIRTEEN

The shadow turned into a very angry Mrs Lionel, who swung at Clive and sent him crashing to the floor. He whimpered, and tried to get up, but she did it again, hitting him across the shoulders with something round and, by the *oooof* Clive emitted as he hit the rug, very heavy. Quicker than an eighty-two-year-old woman should really move, Mrs Lionel grabbed a dining table chair and squeezed it over the man, sitting down once it was stable to trap him.

Rosemary sat up, pulling at the collar of her dress, and feeling her tender neck. 'What on earth did you hit him with?'

Mrs Lionel held the object aloft.

'My pudding.'

'Yes, dear.' Mrs Lionel peeled back a section of the calico. 'It seems to have crumbled. I told you there were too many breadcrumbs in it.' She sat the pudding on her lap. 'Never mind. Luckily, I have a perfectly good one hanging in my home for lunch tomorrow.' She leaned over slightly to look at the mess of letters on the floor. 'Are these from Alasdair?'

'Yes. He sends them twice a year: Christmas and my birthday.'

'And you've never read them?'

Rosemary said nothing.

Mrs Lionel smiled and sat straight, make the chair skid a little and Clive groan. 'I think, dear, that *not* reading them is a perfectly good idea for now.'

Rosemary clambered up and straightened the skirt of her dress. 'I'm lucky I have you,' she said to her friend.

'Yes, dear.' Mrs Lionel plumped her hair. 'You are.'

———

CHRISTMAS DAY DAWNED PEACEFULLY in Mulbury. The sirens and shouts that had signalled the end of Christmas Eve and Clive's treachery had long gone. Rosemary lay in her bed, staring out through the window, Sunny in a comfortable curl at her feet. She couldn't shake the vision of Jasper Lu looking in horror at the bruises on her neck as the hullabaloo died down. She touched them now, knowing that they would be an uncomfortable reminder of being squashed by Clive for days to come as they changed colour and vowed to wear her hair out of its braid until they were gone. 'Lucky it's cooled down,' she said to Sunny.

The cat put a striped leg across her closed eyes. *Let me sleep,* she seemed to say. *It's been a hard few days.*

It was a relief to fling open the windows and doors to feel the change in the weather. Rosemary showered and dressed in a slim shirt and long skirt while standing next to the fly screen in her bedroom to let a cool breeze play across her skin. Outside, chickens scratched contentedly in their yard while fat white ducks waddled across to the pond. A magpie sat on the railing of the balcony, and warbled loudly, making Sunny finally put her head up and yawn. Rosemary brushed her hair, letting it fall loosely down her back, and headed for the kitchen.

Mrs Lionel was the first to arrive for Christmas lunch. She sat a basket on the table and pulled a perfect Christmas pudding from its depths. 'We'll put it on to boil later,' she said, balancing it across the top of Rosemary's large saucepan by tying it to a wooden spoon. 'I brought the brandy for the sauce.'

'I got cream from Roman's farmer friend,' said Rosemary. 'He has dairy cows and his other herd.'

'With your turkey and veg, we're going to have a magnificent feast.' Mrs Lionel drew several containers of shortbread from the basket. 'One that we deserve.'

'Did you bring your present from Kris Kringle?'

'What's that, dear?' For a moment, Mrs Lionel looked puzzled. 'Oh, I see. Yes, it's here.' She pulled a present out, a plain brown paper wrapped square with a dazzle of red, green and gold ribbon.

'Any idea what it is?'

Before Mrs Lionel could answer, there was a 'Yoo hoo' from the shop entrance and Rakisha stumbled in, catching at the door and making the bell clang furiously.

'In here,' called Mrs Lionel.

Rakisha appeared, wispy grey coils of long hair about her face. 'Rosemary, darling, that door. Really. Couldn't you get a softer bell, one with a less raucous jangle?'

'No.'

'Oh.' Rakisha clawed the hair from her face. 'Merry Christmas anyway, darlings.'

'You look lovely,' said Mrs Lionel, reaching out to pick up the ends of the long lengths of velvet ribbon falling from Rakisha's shoulders. 'That's the outfit Patti made for you.'

'Yes, darling, only I added some decoration to make it more festive.' She spun around, revealing more cascades of ribbon falling loosely down her back like purple Rapunzel hair.

'Interesting,' said Rosemary.

'So very much so.' Rakisha let the tote bag fall from her shoulder. 'And I've brought a pudding for you, darling Rosemary. I heard yours had a fatal accident.' She handed over a lump of something wrapped in beeswaxed cloth. 'Vegan, of course.'

Rosemary took the pudding, feeling it crumble beneath her fingers and placing it hastily on the kitchen bench.

'Very nice of you, Rakisha,' said Mrs Lionel before Rosemary could comment. 'Thoughtful.'

'Oh, and I bought my Kris Kringly to open.' Rakisha flourished the parcel. 'That's what you said to do, darling Mrs Lionel.'

'Indeed. Why don't you pop it under Rosemary's tree?'

As Rakisha did what she was told, Mrs Lionel held a finger up to Rosemary, who was still eyeballing the gifted pudding. 'Don't say a word,' she whispered.

'Of course not,' Rosemary whispered back as she shifted the crumbling dessert to the kitchen and hid it behind the fruit bowl. 'As if I would.'

'Hmph,' said Mrs Lionel.

Jasper came in next, dressed in a neat navy shirt and new jeans. He slid a bowl onto the bench, smiled at Mrs Lionel and Rakisha, and looked up at Rosemary. She saw him glance at her neck and pulled her hair around to spill across her front. He hesitated, then put his hand out to sweep lightly down the silver streak running from her temple to the ends of her hair. 'Merry Christmas, Rosemary Exeter,' he whispered, stepping in to kiss her cheek before crashing heavily into her as someone pushed him from behind.

'Oh, goodness, sorry, Jasper.' Gerry thumped something on the kitchen bench. 'Patti's loaded me up, and I was completely out of control.' He wiped at his brow and nodded to Jasper and Rosemary. 'Happy Christmas, anyway.'

Jasper smiled. 'Thanks, Gerry. Same to you.'

'Jasper? You can let me go now.'

Jasper turned back to Rosemary, his face deepening with that familiar embarrassed crimson as he realised he was gripping her arms. 'I'm so sorry, Rosemary. I must have grabbed you in case you fell.'

'Right. But I'm not falling so you can let go now.'

He dropped his hands away. 'Oh. Sorry.'

She looked into his deep eyes and, before she could think too much about it, returned his kiss. 'Merry Christmas, Jasper.'

If crimson had been the colour before, his cheeks were scarlet-fever-red now. She chuckled, patted his forearm, and turned to the rest of her guests before she did anything else foolish.

Kelly was the last to arrive, sauntering in with her chin up, staring around at Rosemary's living area as if to check it out for anything new. Finding nothing but the familiar furnishings and Sunny watching her balefully from her windowsill, she dropped a package under the tree and brandished another at Rosemary. 'Pudding,' she said. 'Heard yours was a disaster.'

'*Met* with disaster,' said Rosemary. 'Not in itself a disaster.'

'Same thing, really.' Kelly glared at her host. 'Anyway, Merry Christmas.'

'And to you,' said Rosemary, channelling the best of Mrs Lionel and plastering a smile on her face.

Kelly turned to view the small crowd. 'No Franco?'

'He had a series of phone calls from France. He might be over later.'

'I see.' Kelly scanned the room. 'Well. I must not take up your time. No doubt you'll have a bit to do.' She turned toward Patti, waggling her fingers over her shoulder at Rosemary as she did. Rosemary resisted the urge to bite them.

'Keeping it civil, dear?' said Mrs Lionel, placing cutlery on the table.

'Yes.' Rosemary widened her eyes at her friend. 'I'm under control.'

'Good.' Mrs Lionel indicated the kitchen. 'Ready, then?'

Rosemary served lunch to the Mulburians amid exclamations of happiness. She didn't think it was the roast turkey, more that the weather was pleasant and a murder mystery solved. Through her open glass doors, the outside noises of distant choughs and the closer songs of Rufous whistlers filtered in, comfortably mixing with the clatter of knives on plates, the laughter at ridiculous cracker jokes, and a good deal of tale-telling that started with Patti's find of a Fair Isle jumper in the gutter to Jasper's revelation that he'd never eaten turkey before coming to Mulbury. She listened, contentment washing over her like a sudden spring rain shower.

'Before we have pudding,' said Gerry, pushing his empty plate away, 'although I can hardly wait for that, should we open up our surprise gifts? The ones that have been perplexing us for several days now.' He rubbed his hands together. 'Then we can take a guess at who the Kris Kringle is.'

'It's clearly Franco,' said Kelly, sipping a glass of Chardonnay. 'He knew he wouldn't make it, so he's given us presents.'

'Well,' said Patti, 'that would be lovely, but we're also missing Roman and Jules and all the others who've gone away for Christmas. Maybe those sweeties left us something?'

'But how did the presents get to our doorknobs, darling?' Rakisha flicked her hair over her shoulder so strands of it caught on Jasper, who was sitting next to her. 'If they were already away, who hung our gifts? No, it's someone who stayed behind.' She pointed her finger at each person at the table in turn. 'Someone at this table.'

Jasper stood and went to Rosemary's olive Christmas tree. 'There's only one real way to find out. Let's open them.' He gathered the parcels in his arms and put them on the table to hand out. There was an excited crinkling of paper as it was torn off the gifts and then sudden silence.

'Ah,' said Mrs Lionel. 'More calico for my next pudding. That will be very useful. What do you have, Patti?'

'Oh,' said Patti. 'How could anyone know that was exactly what I wanted?' She held up a sheath of silken thread that glinted gold and sunset red in the light. 'Look, Gerry. Aren't they beautiful?'

Gerry had his head down and didn't answer. 'My word,' he said. 'This is quite remarkable.' He gazed at the woollen tea cosy lying on the paper in front of him. 'I am definitely not going to shrink this one.'

'Rakisha?' said Patti, leaning over to grasp the woman's hand. 'Are you alright?'

'Oh, yes, darling. Yes, yes.' Rakisha rocked in her chair,

clutching a long, tapered wooden rod to her chest. 'Doesn't this take you back to the days when your mother made porridge on the stove in winter and life was free and always sunny?'

'Isn't that a Scottish spurtle?' Gerry leaned forward to have a better look. 'Was your mother Scottish?'

'Cornish, actually, darling. But we always had one of these. She used it all the time. Oh!' She hugged the implement harder. 'I can stir my oatmeal biscuits as vigorously as I like with this.'

'Is that why they taste like crumbly rocks?' said Kelly.

Rakisha narrowed her eyes at Kelly. 'Well, darling, they sell. People clearly love naturally sweet, wholesome produce.' She pointed her chin. 'What did the Kristy bring you?'

'Well, I'm astonished, actually.' Kelly lifted a ceramic Staffordshire Bull Terrier for all to see. 'It's Pudge, my old dog. It's really quite beautiful.' She wiped her eye as she lowered the statue into her lap.

'What about you, Jasper?' Gerry leaned back in his chair. 'You're never one to make a fuss but I don't see you sharing your gift.'

Jasper hooked hair behind his ear before covering his present back up in its paper. 'No, I won't share. But thank you, whoever it was who gave it to me.'

'Ooooo, really, darling?' Rakisha tried to pluck the present from Jasper, but the bookshop owner had a firm grip on it. 'A secret that will remain a secret?'

Jasper scraped his chair back and went to his bag, slipping the present inside. He turned to the waiting table. 'I think I'll help Rosemary with the pudding.'

'Not until she shows us what she has,' said Kelly.

Rosemary stood slowly and lifted her present from the

table. It was a slender lacquered box, just the right size to store a dozen unopened letters.

'Nice,' said Gerry. 'Useful. Is it what you needed?'

'Yes.' Rosemary tightened her grip on the box. 'Yes, it is. Excuse me while I get dessert ready.' She sat her present on the sideboard and went to the kitchen, where Jasper stood drumming his fingers on the counter.

'Which one?' He swept his hand over the range of puddings on the bench. 'You have a plethora.'

'A plethora of puddings.' Rosemary pointed to the stove. 'But only one to choose from. Mrs Lionel's has been on the boil throughout lunch.'

'Simple decision then.' Jasper snatched a look at her, then dropped his eyes to the cupboard below the bench. 'I'll put out the bowls.'

'Jasper,' said Rosemary softly, 'what was your present?'

He crouched and stuck his head in the cupboard so that his answer echoed into it. 'Perfect.'

'What did you say?'

He stood, a stack of bowls in his hands, and gave her a shy grin. 'My present was perfect.'

As he wandered off to set the table, Mrs Lionel came to inspect the pudding, poking at it so that it swam a little in its boiling water. 'Almost ready,' she said as Rosemary stood next to her.

'Thank you,' said Rosemary.

'Oh, I always make pudding, dear. No need to thank me.'

'Not for the pudding, although I am pleased that you made one.' Rosemary touched Mrs Lionel's arm. 'Thank you for the gift.'

'Gift? I haven't given you a gift.'

'You have, Kris Kringle.'

Mrs Lionel smiled into the pudding water. 'Ah. You think it was me.'

'I *know* it was you. You gave everyone something they wanted.'

The older woman shrugged. 'Well, it's easy enough when you get to know our Mulburians. Most of us are quite transparent.'

'You gave yourself squares of calico.'

'Yes. I'd forgotten I'd even had them, so it was a pleasant surprise.'

Behind them, Gerry read his cracker pun, and the diners moaned and chuckled. Jasper leaned over the little man to look more closely at the joke, catching Rosemary's eye as he did and beaming at her.

Rosemary turned back to Mrs Lionel. 'And Jasper? What did you give him that made him so happy?'

'Jasper, yes.' Mrs Lionel lifted the pudding from its bath and set it gently on a board to unwrap. 'His present was the easiest of all.'

'What was it?'

'Can't you guess?'

'I have no idea.'

Mrs Lionel cut the string on the pudding bag and pulled the calico back to reveal a perfect Christmas pudding. She lifted it onto a plate ready for its brandy burning, then put her hand on Rosemary's arm. 'I gave him a photograph of you.'

The table occupants laughed again; a merry sound as warm as the pudding in front of them. Rosemary felt something press against her leg and there was Sunny, rubbing her cheek on her mistress, and looking very smug. Rosemary swooped her up, and the cat nestled under her chin. Jasper came back to the kitchen to carry the pudding in, pausing to allow Mrs Lionel to smother it with brandy and then set a match to it. The pudding blazed blue, and the table ooooed and ahhhhed.

'And there we have another Christmas, Sunny,' Rosemary murmured to her pet.

The cat stretched a paw out to the scraps of dinner left on a plate on the bench. *Lovely,* she seemed to say. *Now, can I have some turkey?*

ACKNOWLEDGMENTS

Thanks to the dedicated team of volunteer fire fighters who look after us every summer. Not everyone dresses up as Santa! I hope you get that new truck.

All errors are entirely my own.

A Sticky Situation: #1 Mulbury Mystery

When Mrs Lionel discovers the body of an old man under The Exceptional Tree, everyone in the town of Mulbury assumes that he died peacefully. Everyone, that is, except Rosemary who doesn't think the old man's death was particularly peaceful, not when no one has ever seen the man before in a town where everyone knows everyone else.

Rosemary starts a careful investigation, aided (and sometimes hindered) by her fellow shopkeepers on Goldmarket Road.

A small-town mystery with quirky residents and an unimpressed cat.

ABOUT THE AUTHOR

Juno Harvey lives in Victoria, Australia, with her family. She makes jam on the weekends and works in a university during the week.

Want to join Juno's Reader's Team?
Go to www.junoharvey.com and receive a free book!

https://www.junoharvey.com/

Books of light...and shade.